DANNY ORLIS
AND THE
COLORADO CHALLENGE

DANNY ORLIS

AND THE
COLORADO CHALLENGE

BERNARD PALMER

Please note that several books in the Danny Orlis series are published by Sword of the Lord Publications and are available for purchase on their website, www.swordbooks.com.

CONTENTS

CHAPTER 1

DO WE HAVE TO MOVE?

Del Davis, one of the triplets who made their home with Danny and Kay Orlis, took a piece of meat as the plate passed and cut it mechanically. Gloom chased the usual smile from his lips and darkened his young face with a deep frown. He had known all about the call Danny had to move to Colorado to establish an inter-mission advanced flying school, but he hadn't expected him to take it. Neither had Doug or DeeDee, the other two thirds of the triplets, seated opposite him and also toying with their food dejectedly.

Moving to Fairview from Guatemala after their missionary parents lost their lives almost five years ago had been hard for them. They hadn't expected to move again. They loved it at Fairview, and all their friends were here.

"Danny's got all the flying he can do now," Del

had pointed out hopefully, after first learning about Danny's call. "Besides, he would never leave Dr. Kroeger and the mission without a pilot in this area. That's for sure."

The triplets had agreed on that and taken comfort from it. Danny was away a lot, flying all over the north and to a lot of other places. He went wherever the mission needed him. He loved his work and was sure he was doing what God wanted him to do. They had heard him say so countless times.

"That's not all," sixteen-year-old DeeDee had added confidently. "He knows that we have only one more year of high school left. He'd never think of making us leave Fairview before we graduate."

The boys had been sure of that, too.

However, they were wrong. Danny and Kay not only decided to go to Colorado, but they would also be moving there as soon as school was out. They all talked it over as a family and agreed that Danny should do what he felt the Lord wanted him to do. Still, the triplets were stunned when they thought over what his decision really involved for them.

Doug scarcely could believe it. There at the dining table Danny and Kay were talking about it calmly, as though they were going to a meeting at church or to somebody's house for dinner. They didn't seem to realize what they were doing to him and Del and DeeDee.

"But I thought you'd decided to stay here," Doug reminded them when he could trust himself to speak.

"I had a long talk with Dr. Kroeger this afternoon. He thinks I can do more for the Lord by teaching other pilots than by flying."

Doug's gaze shifted from Danny to the solemn features of his sister. He felt bad enough about leaving Fairview and all their friends at school himself, but he was sure DeeDee dreaded the change even more than he and Del did. She was always with Sandy Cole. They met in the hall before school and were together until the bus took her home in the afternoon. They went to classes together and studied together and ate lunch together. Often, they would be talking on the phone half an hour after DeeDee got home. Leaving Fairview and Sandy was going to be tough for her. Right then she looked as though she was about to cry.

"We can come back here next fall for school, can't we, Danny?" Del asked.

"I'm afraid not."

"There are good schools in Rock Point, so it won't be necessary to split up," Kay broke in. "We're a family now and belong together."

"But we've *got* to be here next year! The coach is building his whole football team around Del!" Doug exclaimed with dismay.

Danny did not reply, but it was obvious that he was not going to change his mind when he was sure he was in God's will. The Davis triplets had lived with him long enough to be well aware of that. They were moving to Colorado as a family. Nobody was going to stay behind.

"Why don't you go and talk to the coach?" one of the guys on the team suggested at school the next day. "He could get the principal or someone on the school board to go with him to talk to Danny. Maybe that would get him to be reasonable."

"It wouldn't do a bit of good." Del had difficulty in keeping down the self-pity. He couldn't see why Danny and Kay had to be so stubborn. He had a great chance to star on next fall's football team. Everybody said that with him in the backfield Fairview was a cinch to win the conference championship.

Del doubted it would do any good, but he decided to try talking to Danny again. At the supper table that night he mentioned his conversation with the team members.

"They're all saying we're sure letting down everyone in Fairview by leaving this summer. Do we have to move?"

Danny's eyes met Del's. "I'm sure they don't understand our situation. It isn't what others want us to do. It's what we believe God wants us to do."

"There are plenty of people right in the church who would let us stay with them, at least until after the football season."

"I'm sure that's true." Danny sipped his coffee. "But Kay and I have talked it over, and we've explained the situation to the three of you. It's best that we all move at the same time."

"You couldn't wait until November?" he persisted.

"I'll have to start instructing students in September. And a lot of preparations have to be made during the summer. There's no way we can postpone moving."

Frustrated, Del dropped the subject and finished the meal in silence.

In the days that followed, the missionary pilot and his wife went ahead with their plans to move to Colorado. They contacted several real estate agents in Rock Point to learn about available housing. Kay began to pack some of the things they wouldn't need until after they moved. The time soon came when they flew to Rock Point to look for a house.

Driving from the airport in a rented car, Danny voiced his concern. "You know, there aren't many places to rent. We might have trouble finding just what we want."

"I know." Kay's voice was thin and wistful. She was more interested in the type of neighborhood they would live in and the kind of school the kids would attend. There were three high schools in Rock Point. Two of them had the reputation of being well disciplined, but the third was known for being wild and disorderly. The triplets were sincere in their faith and had definite convictions about living holy lives, but she knew how easy it is to be swayed by the wrong kind of kids.

Danny reached over and squeezed his wife's hand. "Well, we both know the Lord has work for us here, so He will provide the right place for all of us. He'll lead us to it. Now we must do our part by looking."

The first two real estate firms had nothing available for rent. At the third, a salesman insisted on showing them some homes that were for sale.

"We don't have much money for a down payment," Danny protested.

"The house I want to show you won't take much money. You'll be surprised how little is needed."

"It will have to be low, or we're wasting your time and ours, too."

The homes they were shown were large and elaborate and priced accordingly.

"I guess they don't know about a missionary's house allowance," Danny said when he and Kay were alone. "The payments on that last house would be more than double the amount. Even if we were foolish enough to try, we wouldn't be able to get a loan as large as that."

The next two realtors they visited had nothing for rent except an apartment or two which obviously did not meet their needs. They had a few homes listed that sounded cheap, but they were not in a respectable part of town.

Kay was discouraged. "I don't mind for ourselves. We could manage in a small place in a rundown neighborhood. But we have the triplets to think about."

Wherever they went the answer was the same. There were plenty of expensive houses, but the few places that had a reasonable rent were scarcely livable.

When they had exhausted the list of realtors, Danny suggested they call on the only pastor in Rock Point that they knew.

"If the realtors don't know of anything, surely Pastor Sherman wouldn't."

"Maybe not." Danny braked the car to a stop in front of a large brick church. "Only I can't think of anything else to do."

The minister shook their hands warmly and invited them into his study. "I've been trying to get hold of you all day."

"You've never even met us!" Danny exclaimed in surprise.

"I know, but we share a mutual friend who told me that you're moving here. He's on the board that invited you to come here and head up the advanced flight instruction for missionary pilots. Dr. Norton used to attend our church when we were in Denver." The minister spoke in a tone of suppressed excitement. "I tried to call you when I learned you were coming here today. I even called the realtors, but I was a couple of steps behind you. Tell me, did you find a house?"

"Not yet. We're beginning to think there isn't a house in Rock Point that's even halfway suitable that we can afford."

"Don't be too sure of that. One of our members is being transferred and wants to sell his house."

Danny interrupted apologetically. "We hadn't planned on buying."

The pastor picked up a pen and tapped his desk rapidly. "I told him I didn't know if you were in a position to buy, but I do think you'd be wise to go and look at it."

They left the church and rode in the pastor's car to a fashionable district not far away.

Danny noted the size of the homes. "This looks like an exclusive part of town. There's no use in our going into one of these homes. We could never afford a place like these."

The minister turned the car into a tree-lined avenue. "We're almost there, Danny. At least take a look at it."

Danny and Kay did not protest, but they already knew that they could not afford a home in such a neighborhood. The well-kept houses on either side of the wide, winding street were brick with two- and three-car garages.

The pastor slowed before a sprawling ranch house of frame construction. "Well, this is it."

The minister pulled over to the curb and shut off the engine. For a moment he waited silently while they stared at the building.

The house, well back from the street, stretched across a beautifully landscaped lot. It did not appear to be as large as some of the places they had looked at, but the neighborhood was more exclusive. In spite of that, it had a comfortable, lived-in look about it, the sort of house that seemed to invite guests to come in and enjoy themselves.

"Like it?"

"Oh, sure." Danny laughed. "Who wouldn't like it? But it's not for us. We can't afford a place like this."

Pastor Sherman got out of the car and led them to the door. He introduced the Orlises to Mr. and Mrs. Owens, who took them on a quick tour of the house. It was even larger than either Danny or Kay had thought it was. There were three bedrooms on the main floor and two bedrooms and a family room in the basement. Most of the house had been redecorated within the last year. Mrs. Owens turned questioningly to Kay.

"It's beautiful," she said, "but we could never afford a place like this."

Joe Owens led them to the living room. "That's what we wanted to talk with you about. Mable and I have been discussing the matter since Pastor Sherman called and asked about bringing you over to look at it. Do you think the house is adequate?"

"It's more than adequate," Danny assured him. "But it's like Kay said. We could never afford a place like this. Not on our missionary allowance."

"You might be surprised. We'll let you have it one of two ways. You can buy it and assume our low-interest loan, or you can rent it for two years with an option to buy at any time during that period. And, if you should decide to buy, we'll figure the rent you paid as payments against the principal and interest as though you bought it today."

"That part sounds fair enough, but–"

"Are you worrying about the amount of rent? What would you say to the same figure the mission board allows you for housing?"

Danny couldn't believe he heard him correctly. "You couldn't possibly come out on a rental figure like that."

"Who's worrying about that? The difference between what we're charging you and what other homes like this rent for is to be our contribution to the Lord's work."

Kay's eyes filled, and tears tumbled down her cheeks.

"I'm sorry," she said when she could speak, "but I've been so concerned about finding a place in a neighborhood that would be good for the children. Everything we had looked at was too expensive or in an area that wouldn't do at all. Now that you offer us this, I'm overwhelmed."

Mable Owen's smile showed that she understood.

CHAPTER 2

YOU CAN'T LEAVE NOW!

When Danny and Kay got back to Fairview from Rock Point, Sandy was at the house with DeeDee. They seemed surprised to see them.

"We didn't expect you so soon," DeeDee said.

"There was no need to stay longer." Excitement shone in Kay's smiling face. "Should I tell her, Danny?"

"Tell me what?"

"We found the loveliest home in one of the nicest parts of Rock Point. It's owned by a Christian couple, and they're renting it to us at a price we can afford. I can't wait until you and the boys see it."

DeeDee's eyebrows bent darkly. She and Sandy had been talking about that very thing a few minutes before. They had hoped that Danny and Kay would have trouble locating a house in Colorado, at least for several months, so that they might be able to start school at Fairview High in the fall.

If they did that, she had reasoned, there would be a possibility that Kay would stay in Minnesota with her and the boys, at least through the first semester. She and Sandy both wanted it to happen so badly! Now, however, a house had been found, and the family would move right away.

"Big deal!" The words burst from DeeDee's lips. She hadn't meant to sound so bitter.

Kay was startled. DeeDee had seemed adjusted to the idea of moving when they talked last. She had hoped everything was all right with her.

"I thought we agreed that moving to Rock Point was God's will."

The girl winced. "I'm sorry, Kay. I didn't mean to sound so–so upset. It's just that I didn't think we were going to move so quickly. I hoped we'd stay here in Fairview for most of the summer, at least."

"We were all aware that might happen," Kay said, "but God decided otherwise. And He's given us such a lovely house."

Kay went on to tell DeeDee about the house they would be living in when they moved to Rock Point, sketching the floor plan on a piece of paper and describing the room she thought DeeDee would like. Much of the joy and excitement was gone, however. She even found her own enthusiasm waning. When she and Danny were alone, she confided her uneasiness to him.

"I thought our problems with the triplets were

over as far as moving is concerned, but DeeDee's terribly upset about it."

He loosened a shoe and slipped it off.

"I'm disturbed about the boys, too. We may have some real adjustment problems with them before they settle down to life at Rock Point."

A weak sigh escaped her lips. "And I thought our problems in moving were over when we found a place to live."

Doug and Del were only slightly more interested in the house they were going to live in than their sister had been. They wanted to know if there was room to play ping pong and other games in the basement and how far it was to the church and school. It seemed that Danny and Kay did not have definite answers to their questions.

"We were so excited about getting such a nice place that we didn't think to check all those things," Danny said, "but I wouldn't get upset if I were you. If you do have quite a distance to walk, it'll help you to keep in shape for football."

"That reminds me of something else," Doug put in. "What kind of a team does Rock Point have?"

Danny shrugged. "You could get three answers to that question, the way I understand it."

"What do you mean?" Del was irritated.

"They've got three high schools. There's Rock Point, Central, and Northwest; and all three have football teams."

"Which one will we be going to? That's what I want to know."

"I'm not sure, but I think you'll be going to Northwest. It's the newest school and the biggest, and I think it's the closest to the place where we'll be living." He paused. "I've got to call Pastor Sherman in a couple of days. I'll ask him about it."

Del's imagination was aroused. "Wouldn't it be great to play football for a big school? I'll bet they've got a stadium and everything."

"Yeh?" Doug was scowling. "And maybe they've got all the football players they can use, too. Did you ever think of that?"

* * *

Danny and Kay were busy from morning to night getting ready to move. There was the services of a moving van to secure, clothes and dishes to pack, and a number of items to sell. They didn't like having to sell the horses that belonged to the triplets, but they talked it over as a family and came to the conclusion that there was no other choice.

"We can't take them with us," Danny said. "That's for sure. There's no place to keep three horses in the neighborhood we'll be living in."

Del was more disturbed by that than anyone else. "Couldn't we find someone on the edge of town where we could keep them?"

"I thought of that, but Pastor Sherman said there are so many horses around Rock Point that most of the places are already taken, and those that aren't are too expensive for the average person."

"Uncle Clarence gave them to us," Del protested. "I sure don't like the idea of getting rid of them."

Doug shrugged his shoulders resignedly. "Well, to be really honest, we haven't been giving them all the attention they should have, what with all our school stuff and the trips we've been taking."

DeeDee nodded and glanced at Del. "I feel bad too, Del. But if there's no place for them, at least we can do our best to be sure they get a good home."

* * *

As word spread around school that the triplets were leaving shortly after the first of June, the guys on the football team kept coming to Doug and Del, asking them about it as though there was some chance that the story might be false.

"You're not going to leave Fairview this summer, are you, Del?" a first-string tackle asked. "You're going to stay here and finish school, aren't you?"

"It doesn't look that way." It hurt even to talk about it. "Danny and Kay are moving to Colorado, and we've got to go with them."

His friend groaned audibly. "You can't leave now. We can't get along without you."

Another teammate suggested that they talk Danny and Kay into letting them stay in Fairview and finish high school. "You could live at our house if you want to. It would be okay with my dad. He said yesterday that Danny must have rocks in his head if he takes you two away from here before you've graduated."

Del pulled in a shallow breath and pushed the air from his lungs with a rush. "We already tried that idea, but Danny didn't go for it."

"I don't see why not. He's not your dad."

The Davis boy bristled. It was one thing for him to get uptight about Danny; he guessed he wasn't any different from the other kids when it came to criticizing his parents. But he couldn't let anyone else talk about Danny like that.

"Maybe not," he retorted, "but Danny's the only dad I've got. He and Kay took all three of us in and made a home for us. He seems like my real dad."

"Maybe so, but he sure doesn't act as though he thinks anything of you, jerking you out of high school the way he's doing when the whole football team is depending on you."

"Now that I really think about it," Del said loyally, "I wouldn't want to stay in Fairview without Danny and Kay, and I know Doug and DeeDee feel the same as I do."

DeeDee's friends were as concerned about her leaving as the guys were about Del and Doug. Sandy and Brenda were the most disturbed about it. Neither of them could see how they could possibly get along without Danny and Kay Orlis and DeeDee to help and encourage them.

"I just know I won't be able to live as consistent a Christian life alone as I could if Kay and DeeDee were here," Sandy said forlornly as they met after their last class for that day.

Brenda's face grew serious. "I feel the same as you do about that. It seems as though I've always got to go to one or the other about something."

They went into the little snack shop, The Hitching Post, near school and found a booth at the back.

Sandy took a straw and played with it for a moment. "I don't know whether this is right or not, but I'm going to pray that DeeDee doesn't have to leave now. I can't stand to think about her going away."

Brenda only frowned. She knew they shouldn't depend on DeeDee and Kay to keep them true to Christ, but she knew she would miss DeeDee an awful lot too.

* * *

Doug and Del still were not completely resigned to moving to Colorado. They talked with Danny about it on several occasions, trying to get him to postpone the move.

"Do we *have* to leave as soon as school's out?" Doug wanted to know.

"We'll be here for a week or so after school's out, the way it looks now. We've got to get a lot of work done before we leave here."

Doug shook his head. "That's not what I meant. I thought maybe we could wait until fall."

Danny crossed the room and sat down across from them. He knew how they felt about leaving. He had been through the same thing himself when he was in high school. It hadn't been easy for him then, and it wouldn't be easy for them now. Still there was no other choice open to them as a family – not if they wanted to remain in the will of God.

"I've got to go to Denver on July 1 to take some special training for teaching," he explained. "If we don't move as soon as we can, Kay will have the full responsibility of getting settled. We wouldn't want that, would we?"

Doug's face clouded. "I guess not."

"There's something else Doug and I have been thinking about, Danny," Del put in. "We could have a job with a farmer south of town if we want it. He'd use us all summer."

"Were you thinking you'd like to stay there and work until school starts?" he asked them.

"Not exactly. We couldn't live at the farm. There's no place for us."

"What Del means is that we'd like to stay here and work if you and Kay and DeeDee wait to move until just before school starts. But we don't want to be here and have the rest of you in Colorado."

"I can understand that." Danny smiled warmly at them. "I don't think we'd like to be so far away from you, either." He got to his feet. "I have a couple of ideas that might make it possible for you to move to Rock Point right away and still spend the summer working."

Danny was anxious to have them spend the summer working. He knew they would need the money for school, but there was something else even more important. He wanted them to learn the value of working hard.

The boys eyed each other quizzically. They did want jobs, and they did have the farm jobs offered them. Still, working wasn't the main reason for their interest in taking the jobs. Their real purpose had been to convince Danny that it would be better for them to wait until August to move. They saw now, however, that it was useless for them to try to make him change plans.

"Do you know where we can get work in Colorado?"

"I can't say for sure, but I've got a few contacts out there that we can check out in a couple of days. How about it?"

Del shrugged. "If we've got to move, we may as well get work in Colorado. I sure don't want to spend all summer in a town where I don't know anybody."

* * *

The triplets finished their exams for the year and had to go back to the school building the following Friday morning to pick up their report cards. They ate breakfast somberly that day. It was not going to be easy to see the kids for the last time.

"I sure wish I didn't have to go back there at all," Doug grumbled.

"I don't," DeeDee said. "I promised Brenda and Sandy that I'd meet them and go to the snack shop afterward."

Del pushed his plate aside. "Moving to Rock Point wouldn't be so bad if we could only come back here for school next fall."

The gloom in DeeDee's eyes deepened. "You'd just as well forget that. It isn't possible."

Kay had to go into town that morning, so she drove them out to school and made arrangements to pick them up on the corner in front of the bank at twelve o'clock.

"That will give you a little time to tell everyone goodbye."

Doug scowled. "I'd rather not say goodbye to anyone. If we've got to leave, I'd just as soon go without all of that."

The last day of school was even worse for them than they figured it would be. Several teachers and a lot of the kids crowded around to tell them goodbye.

Del and Doug didn't even remember what they said, but at last they were out of the building and on their way toward the bank.

"I'm glad that's over." Doug exclaimed.

"Only it's not all over. We'll have to go through it again at church the Sunday before we leave."

"That's one Sunday I don't think I'll be there!"

CHAPTER 3

YOUR SUMMER SHOULD BE GREAT!

When the triplets came to breakfast the following morning, Danny and Kay already were sitting at the table. They stopped talking immediately as DeeDee pulled out a chair and sat down.

"Don't let us stop you," DeeDee said.

"From what?"

"From whatever you were talking about just now."

"Oh, that." Danny glanced at her and then at her brothers. "Kay and I were just talking about the phone call I had last night."

The boys sat down and waited for Danny to continue. Danny had a lot of phone calls, especially now that they were getting ready to move, but there was something about the way he had spoken that made them curious.

"And what was it all about?" Del insisted when the silence continued.

Danny grinned. He knew he was intriguing them and wanted to stretch out the good news. "My call was from Mr. Kramer."

"Who's he?" Doug demanded.

"I know!" DeeDee put in. "He's the man who owns the dude ranch up in the hills near Rock Point that you were telling us about."

"That's right. Mr. Kramer's the man I got in touch with about work for you for the summer."

DeeDee inhaled quickly. "And you got work for us?" It didn't seem possible.

"Right! When I called him the first time, he said he would have to get in touch with his new manager to see what the situation was. Well, he phoned back last night and said they could use all three of you. You'll be waitressing in the dining room, DeeDee."

"And what about us?"

"They'll be washing dishes, won't they, Danny?" DeeDee's eyes danced.

"You wouldn't do that to us, would you?"

"I imagine they've got machines for that job. Anyway, they've got something else for you to do. They want you guys to work around the place and take care of the horses."

A smile broke broadly across Del's face. He couldn't ask for anything better than helping with the horses unless it would be taking care of his own horse. And there might be a chance for some riding.

"That sounds great."

On second thought DeeDee wasn't so sure her job would be fun. "I've never waited tables before."

"C'mon, DeeDee. It's nothing to get uptight about," Doug told her. "You've helped Kay plenty around the house."

"That's right, DeeDee," Kay added. "You won't have any problems. In a couple of days you'll feel as though you've been waiting tables all your life."

"Okay, all of you," Danny broke in. "If you'll be quiet a moment. I'll tell you the rest of the good news."

All eyes turned to him intently.

"I also mentioned to Mr. Kramer that it was necessary to sell your horses. When he heard they're well-trained western cowponies that are used to having plenty of teenagers around, he gave me a good offer for them. He can use them for his younger guests. If it's okay with you kids, he'll send up a trailer to get them in a couple of weeks."

Del could hardly believe his ears. It was better than he had hoped. They would be with the horses all summer, and, maybe even after that, they could see them once in a while.

Doug frowned. "I still feel bad about having to tell Uncle Clarence we've sold them."

"Don't worry, Doug. He'll understand the situation. Besides, the money will be added to the savings for your future education." Kay put her hand on his shoulder and hugged DeeDee with her other arm. "The Lord has worked these things out wonderfully. We've got a lot to be thankful for. Your summer should be great!"

A crooked smile flashed across Del's face. "It's going to be a fantastic summer for you, DeeDee," he teased. "Think of all the handsome guys you'll meet. You ought to have a ball."

"Look who's talking. You'll have a crush on every girl in the place."

Surprisingly, Del didn't argue. Danny's eyebrows arched as he glanced at the boys. It was the first time either of them had allowed that subject to come up without a protest!

* * *

The day when Danny, Kay, and the triplets were to leave Fairview bore relentlessly down on them. The three teenagers tried to ignore time as much as possible in the feverish activity of packing and saying goodbye, as though pretending the day wasn't going to arrive could possibly slow its approach. The hours and days marched by with maddening regularity, and the time they were to leave was almost upon them.

There were the inevitable going away parties – lots of them. Brenda and Sandy had a dinner for DeeDee, a tearful little affair at the best restaurant in town.

DeeDee was flattered by their extravagance, but when she got home, she cried half the night.

The guys on the football team had a party for Doug and Del at Larry Larson's home, and the kids at church had another for all three of them.

These sad farewells were hard on the boys as well.

"I wish everyone would forget this party business. It's rough enough to have to move away from here without all of this junk to make it worse," muttered Del one evening after a party.

"Yeh." Doug dropped to the bed and kicked off his shoes. "But I think the parties ought to be about over now. I don't know of anyone else who'll be giving us one, do you?"

"There's one more." Del hung his shirt on the back of a chair. "Sunday night after the service they're going to serve coffee in the basement of the church as a farewell party for all of us."

Doug groaned. "And I thought we wouldn't have to go through anymore."

They knew the parties were held because the kids liked them and wanted to show how sorry they were to have them move away, but that sure didn't make leaving Fairview any easier. Del and Doug both felt like running the other way when anyone began to talk about the move they were making.

At last the farewell at the church was over in a flurry of speeches. The girls cried and followed

DeeDee out to the car. The boys waved their final goodbyes from the rear window.

Danny sighed his relief as they were driving home. "I'm glad that's over."

"So am I," Kay replied. "I've been dreading it all week."

Danny yawned wearily. "I'm glad we're getting home early so we can get a good night's sleep. The van will be here in the morning."

The fact that they actually were going to move the next day didn't seem real to DeeDee. It was as though she had lost the capacity to think or feel and was suspended in a vacuum where there was no such thing as reality. She went to bed at the usual time, but sleep was fitful. She got up before six o'clock the next morning and was sitting in the living room staring out the window when Danny and Kay got up.

However, there was reality for her in the moving van that rumbled to a stop before the Orlis home shortly after eight o'clock that Monday morning. And there was reality in the two burly men who started packing the furniture and hauling it out to the truck. By noon it was loaded and ready to leave.

DeeDee stood with her brothers on the porch of the empty house a moment or two before getting into the car. She didn't feel like saying anything; she didn't think she would ever feel like saying anything.

"Are Sandy and Brenda coming out to tell you goodbye before we go, DeeDee?"

She shook her head. "I told them not to." Her eyes were moist and reddened. "It was hard enough to say goodbye last night. I didn't want to have to go through that again today."

The truck slowly drove out of the yard, and Danny and Kay joined the triplets.

"Come on, kids," Danny said. "We'd better get a move on."

Del spoke for all three of them, his voice catching. "Just a minute, Danny."

"I want to go back in the house just once more," DeeDee said. "Okay?"

Danny nodded. DeeDee always had been the sentimental one in the family. He knew how hard it was for her to make a move like this.

DeeDee turned and went inside. It had been such a happy home. Now, however, without the furniture it looked so different. It was cold and gloomy – even unfriendly. She moved from one room to another looking at the familiar walls with a desperate longing.

There was no doubt about it. The empty house had a sad air in its nakedness, as though it felt a measure of the sorrow that was hers at having to move.

DeeDee crossed the well-worn carpet she had loved so much and opened the door to her room. The ache that seized her was so great she could scarcely breathe. Tears began to stream down her cheeks. She knew it was foolish to cry that way, but she couldn't help it. She was still crying when the outside door opened and Kay came in.

"I'm sorry." She dabbed at her eyes. "I'll be ready to go in a minute."

"I know exactly how you feel." Tenderly Kay put an arm around the girl's trembling shoulders. "It's not easy for any of us to leave a home that has meant so much to all of us."

Kay stood there with her for a while until her crying had spent itself and she was able to wipe away the tears.

"We really have to go now."

Together they left the house and went back to the car. They all knew that DeeDee had been crying, but not even the boys mentioned it. They understood exactly how she felt. They would have had to admit that they felt a little like crying themselves.

* * *

It was late the following evening before they finally arrived in Rock Point, Colorado. The van had arrived several hours ahead of them; and by the time they pulled up in front of their new home, most of the furniture was already unloaded.

DeeDee saw the big expanse of lawn, the two-car garage, and the broad picture window. "Is this the house we'll be living in?"

"That's right." Danny got out and looked around. "Like it?"

DeeDee got out of the car and hurried toward the house. "You tried to tell us what it was like, but I never imagined it would be anything like this."

"Neither did we, but the Lord provided abundantly above all we asked or expected!"

They went into the house and stopped just inside the door to admire the spacious living room.

"This is big enough to play basketball in." Doug exclaimed.

Kay laughed. "I'd better not catch you playing basketball in here."

He went to the center of the room and turned about. "Look at that fireplace! We'll sure have a lot of fun sitting in front of the fire eating popcorn next winter, won't we, Danny?"

"And you and Del will get a double load of fun out of it. It's going to be your job to go out in the hills to buy our firewood and cut it."

Kay crossed the living room, motioning to the rest of the family to follow her. "Don't you want to see the rest of the house? Come and pick out your bedrooms."

The triplets followed her. This was their new home, and Danny and Kay were so excited about the way the Lord had provided it for them. They finally felt like getting into the spirit of it too.

CHAPTER 4

IS THIS REALLY A RANCH?

The triplets thought they would be staying at the house for a few days to help get the boxes unpacked and the dishes and clothes put away, but Danny reminded them that they were expected at the dude ranch immediately to start work.

"Mr. Kramer told me they like to have their summer help on the job as soon as possible. I guess they have quite a lot of business in June."

DeeDee was concerned about Kay having to work alone. "Maybe the boys could go ahead. I'll stay here with Kay until you get the house straightened up and livable."

"Thank you, DeeDee," Kay replied, "but I'll manage. Danny'll be here to help me for a while, and the rest of the work I can do as I get time. I don't think I'm going to have to hurry. It looks as though I'll be alone most of the summer after all."

DeeDee didn't like that either and started to pro-test. Kay knew that she needed the money for school and insisted on her going up to the ranch with the boys. "You'll be able to come home on your days off to visit me and fix up your own room."

"I still feel guilty leaving you this way," DeeDee said.

"Don't worry. I'll help her." Danny laughed. "I don't know how much good I'll be, but I'll be in there pitching."

* * *

The next morning Danny took them up to the ranch in the hills thirty or forty miles west of Rock Point.

The mountains pressed hard against Rock Point from the west, brooding over the sprawling little city. Danny braked to stop at a light, signaled his turn, and moved onto the highway that wound between the mountains and over the pass. Half an hour out of town Danny left the highway and angled up a steep, twisting trail.

DeeDee was stunned to silence by the beauty of the steep, pine-crested hills. She saw deer feeding on the opposite slope and a mountain goat stand-ing imperiously on his commanding vantage point half up the ridge.

Del was the first to speak. "It's going to be great spending all summer out here."

Doug and DeeDee promptly agreed in unison.

The narrow graveled road snaked along the mountainside, leaped the creek on small wooden bridges at half a dozen spots, squeezed through a rustic gate, and came to a halt in front of the new dining hall at the JB ranch. Danny pulled up beside a car with New Jersey plates and stopped.

"Well, here we are."

The triplets remained in the car for a moment, looking about curiously.

The JB was one of the many working cattle ranches in that part of the state, but it had found catering to vacationing easterners more profitable than cattle. They still had the cattle, but the tourists took precedence. The evidence of the transformation was still visible in the mixture of old and new buildings. There was a large house of uncertain age spread along one side of the layout. On the opposite rim stood the barn, a somewhat nondescript building that must have been of the same vintage as the house. There was a bunkhouse, well painted but obviously of another day. Nearby was the foreman's house. It was fairly small but of the same general structure and state of repair as the big house.

The dining hall and lodge were comparatively new, sparkling buildings with long expanses of glass. A huge fireplace filled one end of the carpeted lounge. Guest cabins were discretely scattered about the grounds, affording the measure of privacy well-paying visitors demanded. While Danny and the triplets sat in the car, an ornately dressed couple rode by on a pair of stocky quarter horses.

Del whistled softly. "Did you see that? Those are the best-looking horses I've about ever seen. I wonder where our horses are?"

DeeDee had scarcely seen the horses. She was staring at the riders. "I wonder what Uncle Clarence would say if somebody on his ranch dressed like that?"

Del directed his attention back to Danny. "Is this *really* a ranch?"

"It's not exactly like the Circle R. It's for dudes – people who've never been on a ranch before. But I do think they run some cattle."

Frown lines formed around Del's mouth. "I know that, but I figured it would be a lot more like a real ranch than it is. I didn't know it was going to have a motel with a swimming pool and everything." He paused and pulled in a deep breath. "I sure don't know whether I'm going to like working around here."

The four of them went into the office, and Danny asked to see Mr. Kramer. He was not at the ranch that afternoon, but his manager was there, sitting at his desk in a small room off the lounge. He was a thin, pallid little man who apparently found it impossible to smile. His annoyed attitude complained at the interruption without benefit of words. He adjusted his tie impatiently and shifted the papers around his desk as he inquired about the purpose of their visit.

"I don't know why you didn't get here this morning," Mr. Terrill muttered, signing his name to a letter in an important scrawl. "We always instruct our new people to start work in the morning. That way we can get them acquainted with their duties at a time when our management personnel are not so busy."

The triplets glanced uneasily at each other.

"I'm afraid that's my fault, Mr. Terrill." Danny's voice was gentle but even and firm. "When I talked with Mr. Kramer about the triplets coming out to the ranch to work this summer, I neglected to ask him when they should come out here. I chose a time that was convenient for me. I'm sorry."

Terrill's look narrowed, and then his features seemed to soften. "I see." He picked up the papers on his desk once more and shuffled through them with nervous fingers. "It would have been nice if you had been more considerate, but the harm is done now. We will have to make the best of it."

Del spoke up quickly. "We can wait until morning to start if that would be better for you."

The dyspeptic manager pushed back from his desk and got to his feet. "No, my afternoon's already been ruined by this interruption. We'd just as well go and get this over with."

Danny excused himself and left. With growing concern, the triplets watched him leave. They weren't sure they wanted to be left alone with Mr. Terrill.

The manager of the ranch took DeeDee to the

woman who was in charge of the dining room and introduced the teenager as a new waitress.

"You can show Miss Davis what you expect of her and the hours you want her to work. One of the other girls can take her to her room." With that he pivoted and strode briskly to the door. "You boys can find the foreman around the barn. Tell him I sent you to help with the mowing."

With that, he turned and marched pompously through the door and down the hall to his private office.

Doug and Del left the dining room and walked briskly across the lawn in the direction of the barn. They really wanted to leave the ranch and walk in the direction of Rock Point, but they had been hired to work. They did as they were directed without delay.

"What do you think of Mr. Terrill?" Doug asked.

His brother grinned. "I don't know for sure. He acts as though he's got a stomachache."

"That's not all that's bothering him. I've never seen anyone so sour and disagreeable."

Del had to agree. Mr. Terrill didn't have the most pleasant personality he had ever seen. He hoped they wouldn't be working directly for him.

"It seems to me the foreman is the one who'll be giving us orders."

"I hope you're right. I'm afraid I wouldn't be able to get along with that character very well if I had to have him telling me what to do."

They found the foreman in the barn with two other teenagers who worked at the ranch. The graying man was taller than Danny by half a head. His muscular frame had been beaten thin by long years in the saddle through snow and wind and rain. His well-worn boots and faded Levi's seemed strangely out of place in the plush surroundings of the JB Ranch. The foreman obviously was a carryover from the days when only cattle and tough little cow ponies made up the livelihood of the owners of the JB.

Doug was the spokesman. "We were sent out here to find the foreman."

"Then your task is done, laddie. I'm Scot MacDermott." Kindness tempered the steel in his blue-gray eyes, and his smile was warm. But his square jaw and firm handshake told the boys that they wouldn't want to do anything to kindle his anger against them.

"Mr. Terrill sent us," Doug explained. "He said we were to tell you to put us to work. We were supposed to mow, I guess."

"Ay," Scot said. "I'll see that ye get to work soon now, that I will." The wiry foreman's years in the West had not worn off his Scottish burr. Mixed with a drawl, it made a peculiar accent. "An' I s'pose ye'll be want'in a room, too."

"That would be better than sleeping in the barn," Del put in.

Scot faced him, his features stern; but laughter

winked in his eyes. "And what's wrong with *my* barn, laddie?"

At that moment the boys knew they were going to enjoy working for Scot MacDermott.

In the dining room DeeDee was being introduced to her job by the harried, hawk-faced Miss Gray. As she talked, the woman's gaze fluttered nervously around the empty dining room as though she was envisioning it crowded with unreasonable, complaining guests who weren't being served fast enough to satisfy them.

"I do hope you'll be able to learn quickly, DeeDee." She brushed a stray strand of hair from her eyes with a quick, self-conscious gesture. "Mr. Terrill gets so upset when someone is served the wrong order or has to wait longer than usual. He takes it so personally."

"I'll try my best." Miss Gray's lack of confidence in her torpedoed DeeDee's own assurance that she would be able to handle the job successfully. At that moment she was positive she would remember nothing she had been told and would bring the explosive Mr. Terrill swooping down on both her and the nervous Miss Gray. She didn't know why she had ever taken the job. It would have been better to spend the summer in Rock Point with nothing to do than to be out here where she would have to work for such an unpleasant person as Mr. Terrill. But there was nothing she could do about it now.

Miss Gray showed her around the dining hall,

indicating the tables that were to be her responsibility and warning her again to be sure she made no mistakes. Only then did the supervisor suggest that they go to the room that would be DeeDee's for the summer. They were on their way there when a young busboy swaggered up to them.

"Hi, baby. Where'd you pop in from?"

Indignation flecked the supervisor's voice. "Charles, that's no way to talk to DeeDee."

"Cool it, Carolyn." His contempt was unhidden and made it clear that he didn't have to take orders from her.

"And don't call me Carolyn," she retorted. "My name is Miss Gray."

"Okay, Carolyn. If you want your slaves to call you Miss Gray, it's all right with me. It might help to keep them in line. Don't you think so, baby?"

DeeDee drew away from him. He wasn't the kind of boy she liked, that was sure.

He winked his derision at Miss Gray and grinned in DeeDee's direction. "Welcome to the old rat race. See you around."

Miss Gray's cheeks were crimson. When he was gone, she told DeeDee about him.

"Charles is quite difficult for all of us. He's Mr. Kramer's nephew, and he knows that none of us on the staff have the authority to discharge him." Her sigh was deep. "I know he's one of the reasons that poor Mr. Terrill's ulcer has been acting up lately.

We've seen the change in that man since Charles came to work."

DeeDee's apprehension increased as the time for dinner to be served drew near. She was sure she wouldn't be able to do anything right, and Mr. Terrill would pounce out of the woodwork before she'd finished serving her first customer. She would probably be fired before she had time to learn anything about her job!

DeeDee did make a few mistakes at first. She brought one couple steak when they'd ordered chicken and another coffee when he wanted milk. But, surprisingly, nobody criticized her for it, not even the cook as he changed the entrees.

She apologized for her error.

"Forget it, DeeDee." His smile said more than his words. "You can eat one steak and I'll eat the other."

* * *

The first few days at the ranch were long and quite difficult for the triplets; however, by the time they had put in a week, they were quite accustomed to the routine.

Scot, who had learned from the boys that they had just moved to town, suggested they might want to spend their day off at home.

"It so happens that I'm going to spend the weekend

at my daughter's in Rock Point. I can take you in with me and bring you back on Sunday evening."

Del and Doug accepted eagerly. They rode into town with the foreman and got out in front of the house.

Del stood looking up the drive toward the garage. "I don't believe Danny's home."

"Maybe he's gone to Denver already."

"I sure hope Kay's here. That would really be something if neither of them were around."

At that moment a car slowed and turned in the drive that paralleled theirs. The sleek sedan came to a stop, and both boys stared as the car door opened. A girl about their age got out. She glanced at them appraisingly, her long blond hair framing a smile, and turned away to hurry up the walk with quick, sure movements.

Doug's eyes widened. "Wow!"

On the front steps the girl who lived next door paused, hidden by shadows and shrubbery. Doug couldn't be sure, but he thought he saw her turn to look in their direction.

"Did you see her, Del?" Doug asked when she finally disappeared inside. Awe crept into his voice.

"What do you mean, did I see her? I'm not blind."

Doug shuffled forward, entranced by the vision that had just drifted into the neighboring house. "Isn't she the prettiest girl you ever saw?"

Del faced him. "You've flipped."

Doug was still staring at the house. "Was she real or are we dreaming?"

"That car didn't drive up by itself."

"With a girl like that around, Rock Point can't be all bad."

Del grinned broadly. "Cheer up, Doug. Maybe she has a sister for you."

"Now wait a minute! I saw her first. You can have the sister if she's got one."

Del's laughter burst out. "You know, this is stupid. You've only seen her once. You don't even know her name."

"I saw her first."

"Calm down. She's probably got a dozen guys on the string."

They were still teasing each other as they went into the house. Kay, who was in the living room, looked up curiously. She wondered what they found so amusing, but they didn't tell her.

The boys asked about Danny and learned that he already had gone to Denver to start flight school the following week.

"He was so anxious to get that out of the way," Kay said, "that he decided to start as soon as possible."

Del nodded knowingly. That was how a guy felt about a job he liked. But the work they had to do at the ranch was another matter. He thought he would get to work around their horses, at least some of the time, but the closest he had gotten to a horse was when he stopped the power mower to let one of the guests ride by.

Doug and Del went to Sunday school and church with Kay the following morning. They whistled their surprise when they saw the sprawling, modern structure.

"Wow! How do you find your way around?" Doug asked, measuring the beautiful brick building with his eyes. It seemed almost as big as the high school they had attended in Fairview.

"It's big," agreed Kay, "but the gospel is preached here the same as it was in Fairview."

The boys found seats not far from the door. They never had been in a church even half so large. The rows of seats stretched endlessly down to the pulpit and choir loft. The sanctuary was bigger than the high school auditorium at Fairview – a lot bigger.

Doug leaned over to his brother and whispered, "Our whole congregation back home could sit up with the choir and have a little room left."

CHAPTER 5

IT'S JUST A BIG BLUFF

The dining room at the JB ranch was in that late afternoon hush before the rush of guests. The tables had been set with fresh flowers in the bud vases, the napkins were in place, and Miss Gray had her crew of waitresses ready to go to work.

The dining hall supervisor wandered nervously about the room, touching the tablecloth at one table, rearranging the flowers at another, and hoping Mr. Terrill would be less complaining than usual.

DeeDee had grown accustomed to Miss Gray's fluttering apprehensions of doom, but the ranch manager still frightened her. When Mr. Terrill came around, she withered inside and had to fight the impulse to whirl and flee, although he usually looked past her as though she were invisible. She was standing at her station waiting for the first guests when Chuck Grover sidled over to her.

"Hi, doll." The arrogance in his voice caused her to recoil from him. "What're you doin' tonight?"

"Nothing that would interest you." Her voice was purposely cold and impersonal.

"Now, don't be like that. I get interested easy, real easy, when a lovely chick like you comes around."

A customer sat down at one of her tables, and she gratefully went to wait on him. She hoped Chuck would be gone by the time she finished, but he waited at her station brazenly.

"Come on, don't give me a bad time. What *are* you doin' tonight?"

"Working." DeeDee turned her back toward him.

"I'm working, too. I mean *after* we get off work."

"It's really no concern of yours, but I'm going straight to my room as soon as I finish here."

"How come? Your watchdogs are gone. We can slip out and live a little."

"Watchdogs?"

"Those brothers of yours. They're gone now. If you and I slip out for a couple of beers, who's to know?

DeeDee's cheeks flushed hotly.

"I told you that I'm not going anywhere with you, Chuck Grover; and I mean it, whether Doug and Del are around or not!"

She would have said more, but Miss Gray was staring at her with helpless desperation that asked her to please wait on the couple that just came in and do it before Mr. Terrill noticed they hadn't been taken care of. DeeDee strode quickly away from Chuck.

She went about her work, twin spots of scarlet burning on her cheeks. It wasn't so much what Chuck said that infuriated her, as the way he said it. He could give a smile or a simple remark about the weather a double meaning.

He didn't interest her at all; but even if he had, she wouldn't have gone out with him. She was determined that she wasn't going to date unsaved guys and have the trouble Brenda had in breaking off with Duke. Still, she wished she could make Chuck understand that she didn't want to go out with him without making an enemy of him.

When she got off from work, he was no longer in the dining room. She slipped into her sweater and hurried out into the chilly mountain air. The sun was gone, and darkness had crept over the hills. She was halfway to the staff bunkhouse when an all-too-familiar voice stopped her.

"DeeDee!"

She shivered and hurried on.

"Wait a minute!" Chuck followed her. "I want to talk to you!"

She came to a halt and faced him.

A pleased grin bent the corners of his mouth. "Surprise, surprise. It's me."

"I'm quite aware of that." Her tense voice warned him that her attitude had not changed.

"Aren't you even going to talk to me?"

She shrugged her slim shoulders. "What do you want?"

"Nothing much. I just came over to keep you company for a while, that's all."

"You don't listen very well, Chuck. I'm not going anywhere with you."

"It's awful dark for a pretty little girl like you to be out walking alone."

"I'm quite able to take care of myself, thank you."

"I'll behave. I promise. Why won't you go out with me?" His words were more a dare than a question.

DeeDee frowned and looked away. In the dining hall she had promised herself she would explain to Chuck that being a Christian kept her from going out with him. But Miss Gray had been hovering nearby and guests had begun to gather, so she had had a good excuse for keeping quiet. Now, however, they were alone. There was no reason not to tell him, save her own embarrassment.

She squinted at Chuck in the darkness, words clogging her throat. The sound of a car approaching broke the silence. Twin lights came into view, splitting the gloom of the night, and turned in to stop beside the main lodge.

"Why *won't* you go with me?" Chuck persisted. "Are you already dating someone?"

"Well, not actually." DeeDee paused. It wasn't going to be easy, but she had to tell Chuck. She breathed a quick prayer for help; and then, finding courage she didn't know she had, she began. "There *is* a reason why I can't go with you, Chuck. I'm a Christian. I mean, I've put my trust in the Lord Jesus Christ and–"

He glared at her with a lance-like stare. "What?"

"Like I said, Chuck! I belong to the Lord Jesus and want to do only what pleases Him. After all, He died for me–"

"Wait a minute! You, a religious nut? I can't believe it."

DeeDee was glad for the darkness that hid her reddened face and trembling hands. "No, not one of those, but I do love God and believe in His Word and try to obey it. You need to know Him, too. 'For God so loved the world He gave–'"

"A fanatic, a real fanatic!" Chuck snickered scornfully. "Turn it off! I've heard all that gospel stuff already and it's just a big bluff. You'll see things my way with enough of the right persuasion, just like others have." He leaned toward her. "I always get what I want."

DeeDee stumbled backward in surprise. She had not expected this reaction from him.

He grabbed her arm. "Forget that religious act, DeeDee. You're missing all the fun in life. I could teach you a lot."

"No, I am not." DeeDee jerked loose from his grip. "You're the one who's missing out on the best." She whirled away and ran toward the bunkhouse, his mocking laughter ringing in her ears.

* * *

Doug and Del had enjoyed their weekend in Rock Point with Kay. They felt slightly reluctant to go back to the ranch, but they had their bags packed and ready when Scot drove up in front of the house Sunday evening.

Kay went to the door with them. "Tell DeeDee I'll try to drive up to see her – and you boys too – sometime soon. I hope she's also doing fine at her job."

A smile slid across Doug's face. "You might even bring some cookies if you think about it." He started out the door then turned back. "And you don't know the neighbors' names yet?"

"I don't know their names."

"I've got a notion to let Del go back to the ranch without me. I could stick around a few days to help you get acquainted with some people in the neighborhood."

Scot honked the horn, and Doug turned and ran toward the car.

The next few days were busy ones, and the boys had little time to talk to DeeDee.

Mr. Terrill's nervousness increased. He seemed to be everywhere, striding about, impatient and complaining. "Mr. Kramer will be coming out one of these days. The yard will have to be gone over carefully, and the barn must be spotless – absolutely spotless. Mr. Kramer can't stand dirt, and neither can I."

Scot was courteous but obviously unimpressed. "Ay, we'll take care of it in good time, me and the boys."

Mr. Terrill glanced at his watch as though to indicate that the foreman already was wasting valuable time. "I'm sure you realize the importance of having everything in perfect condition when Mr. Kramer arrives. After all, he *is* the owner."

"That I know, Mr. Terrill." The Scottish burr stretched out the name and rolled it across Scot's tongue. "Kramer and me used to ride herd together and eat out of the same can of beans."

Terrill snorted peevishly and stormed back to the house. Scot put the boys on the mowers that morning and had them do nothing else until the vast lawn was closely clipped and immaculate. He had to take a trail ride into the hills for two days, but before leaving he told them to clean the barn thoroughly.

"And mind ye, do a good job or I'll be on the necks of the whole lot of you!"

Doug turned to Andy Madison who was working with them. "He's a great guy."

The other teen nodded. "But he really can lose his cool if he tells a guy to do something and it isn't done."

The boys worked steadily until the barn and the horse sheds were thoroughly cleaned. Not convinced that they could work satisfactorily without supervision, Mr. Terrill swooped out of his office twice each day to inspect what they were doing.

"We must have everything in order when Mr.

Kramer comes." He pranced into a box stall, inspecting the floor and the walls with his eyes. "We want him to see that we're running a tight ship."

Scot, on his return, was pleased. "Ye did a good job."

"Only, I'm getting tired of riding a power mower," Del protested.

The foreman's eyelids slitted. "Work's work, laddie. Some's more fun than the rest, but it all has to be done."

"I thought I was going to get to work with the horses."

Scot folded his deeply tanned arms. "Did anybody tell you that?"

Del shook his head. "But I've had a lot of experience with horses, and I figured maybe I'd get to do something with them."

Scot's laughter rang out across the corral. "Ye have been, laddie. Ye just finished cleanin' out the horse shed."

* * *

Danny started his studies at the flight school the first Monday in July. He found it strange to attend classes and take instruction after all his years of flying. The ground-school work was difficult at first. For one thing, he wasn't used to studying. For another, theory of instruction was a new field for him. He knew the practical aspects of flying, but how to teach them to others was something else.

He enjoyed the airtime much more than the studying. He had spent more hours flying cross-country than he could remember without checking his log and was experienced with two-way radio and flying to radio-controlled airports. He had his multi-engine endorsement and instrument rating.

Danny was amused at having to practice landing in restricted areas. He'd been doing that since the day he soloed. None of the missionary airstrips had excess room, it seemed, except some of Canada's big lakes.

He had to spend some time on maneuvers, learning to pull the plane out of a spin and any other unusual situation a student might blunder into. He had to learn to fly the aircraft from the right seat so his students could be in the normal pilot position. That took a little getting used to, as all the references were different. But, with each passing day, he drew closer to the time when he would have his instructor's rating and be ready to launch the school for missionary pilots. When he wrote home, his messages were full of ideas for the future school.

CHAPTER 6

WHAT'S BUGGING HER?

Chuck's taunting attitude toward DeeDee after she witnessed to him increased steadily. Her presence seemed to irritate him, yet he would deliberately go out of his way to confront her with annoying remarks and ridicule.

One morning he blocked her way as she was hurrying to the lodge to start work.

"I know why Uncle Wally hired you and those brothers of yours this summer!"

"I don't know what you mean. I don't even know your Uncle Wally." DeeDee was defensive instantly.

"Don't lie to me. You're such a good Christian, you wouldn't do that – much!"

"I've told you the truth."

"I heard old Terrill complaining that Uncle Wally himself hired three kids of some missionary friend of his and sent them out here to work, so don't try to tell me you don't know him. He's got some plan cooked up with you to convert his black sheep nephew, right? It's so obvious, it stinks."

"I didn't even know your uncle is a Christian." DeeDee was pleased by this news, in spite of its source. Mr. Kramer probably was not such a mean boss as Mr. Terrill implied. She felt encouraged, even about Chuck. "We're not in on any plan like that, but you do need to know Christ."

Chuck shook his fist close to her face. "You're not fooling me. You'll regret you ever came here."

* * *

The following noon many of the guests were gone on trail rides, and there was little for the dining room staff to do. Chuck sauntered over to DeeDee and another teenage waitress, who were sitting by the side windows.

"Hi, baby."

The girls broke off their conversation and looked up.

"How about a cigarette?" He pulled a pack out of his shirt pocket.

Maxine Engle took one and held it between her lips for Chuck's match.

"Come on, DeeDee, aren't you smoking today?" He held the pack out to her.

"She doesn't smoke."

"Oh? Since when?"

"I never have smoked." DeeDee blushed in confusion.

His laughter was taunting. "Don't worry, doll. If you want people to believe you're such a saint that you don't even smoke, I'm not going to tell on you. Your secret's safe with me."

DeeDee saw the flicker of doubt in Maxine's eyes. Her friend wasn't sure whom to believe. And it would not do DeeDee any good to deny the implication he was making. That would only cause doubts to increase. DeeDee felt so helpless. He would have to do this just when Maxine was starting to show some real interest in talking about spiritual things.

She looked at Chuck. His face gleamed with amusement. It was all a big joke to him.

"I'm giving you the facts about DeeDee," he continued. "You may not know it, but she's such a holy Christian, she doesn't do anything wrong. If you don't believe it, just ask her."

DeeDee's lips trembled as she struggled to control her anger.

"Isn't that right?" he prodded.

"Please, Chuck!"

"She's the one who told me–"

A customer sauntered in, and DeeDee jumped up to wait on him. Chuck's voice floated after her. Anyone nearby could have heard him.

It wouldn't have been quite so bad if he had quit then, but he continued to snipe at her with crude remarks, like a nasty little terrier snipping irritably at her heels, every time they passed in the dining room. She tried to avoid him, but that was impossible. When she finally got off work, she couldn't maintain her composure another moment. She left the dining room in tears and was running across the lawn to the staff bunkhouse when Doug called after her.

"Hi, DeeDee. Got a moment?"

She stopped but didn't look directly at him, trying to keep him from seeing the tears on her face. But she should have known she couldn't do that. He knew her almost as well as he knew himself and saw, instantly, that she was upset.

"What's the matter? Did you get some bad news?"

"Of course not."

"What is it then?"

"How many times do I have to tell you there's nothing wrong. Just leave me alone!"

She left him standing there, staring bewilderedly after her. He was still worried about her when he entered the room he and Del shared.

"Have you talked to DeeDee lately?" he asked his brother.

"Not much."

"Would you happen to know what's bugging her?"

"Maybe some guy stood her up."

"She was bawling when I saw her just now, but she wouldn't tell me what's wrong."

Del put down the magazine he had been reading.

"If some character's bothering her, he'll have to answer to me."

"He'll have to answer to both of us."

Del turned his wrist to catch the time. "Let's go over and talk to her."

"Not now. She won't tell us anything while she's upset."

The boys tried to see DeeDee the following morning after breakfast, but Mr. Terrill cornered them and ordered them out to work.

"Mr. Kramer is going to be here this afternoon. We must have everything in shape." Terrill's desperate tone knifed at them. Before the boys could reply, he skittered away.

As they went about their work, Del and Doug wondered what kind of a man Danny's ranch-owner friend actually was. Judging by the way Mr. Terrill acted, they decided the big boss had to be a hard-hearted slavedriver. But when he came in his battered pickup and run-down boots, they saw he was mild and quiet. He reminded the boys of Danny's dad, Carl Orlis, although he was probably several years younger. He certainly was not the sort of person to be so afraid of.

Mr. Kramer strolled around the grounds for an hour or more, casually talking first with one person and then another. He didn't miss much at the ranch, that was certain; but he wasn't out to find trouble.

Mr. Terrill came out to the shed where several

of the boys were working. The manager was more relaxed than they had ever seen him.

"Mr. Kramer was well pleased with the way he found the ranch. In fact he was almost complimentary." A certain awe crept into his voice as though he couldn't quite believe it was possible. "To show you all how much I appreciate your efforts, I'm going to give you tomorrow afternoon off. You can go on a trail ride, swim, or do anything you wish."

When the ranch manager was gone, Del turned to Madison. "Old Terrill is human after all."

"He's not a bad egg when you get to know him. He barks a lot, but he doesn't bite much."

"I never thought he'd give us credit for doing anything right."

The two boys picked up their pitchforks and returned to their work.

Doug joined them. "What're we going to do tomorrow afternoon? Any ideas?"

"How about a trail ride? We haven't been on a horse since we got here."

Andy was agreeable. "Sounds great to me. I've got a buddy who will want to go along, and there might be some others by tomorrow afternoon."

Doug and Del had known Andy since they started working at the JB ranch. He lived in Rock Point and went to the same school the triplets would be attending. There were a few other young staff members who did also. The full work schedule kept them from getting well acquainted. Doug and Del were glad for this chance to get to know some of them better.

They discussed the plans for the trail ride with Andy as they worked, finally settling on a ride to an old ghost town some of the guests found interesting.

"Say, who's this guy you want to take along tomorrow?" asked Del.

Andy looked up in surprise. "I thought you'd know. He's Chuck Grover, Mr. Kramer's nephew. He works with your sister in the dining room."

"You mean that guy with the long curly hair?"

"Yeh. I thought your sister would've told you all about him by now."

"She's never even mentioned him."

"That's funny. Chuck told me he could get DeeDee to go out with him any time he wanted. He'll probably bring her along for the trail ride."

CHAPTER 7

WHO SAID I HAD A DATE?

Doug and Del sauntered up the steep slope in the direction of the main lodge.

"I wish I knew what was bothering DeeDee so much last night."

"Me, too." Del stooped to pick up a crumpled paper that had been thrown away by one of the guests. "The way Andy was talking, I wouldn't be surprised that Chuck Grover had something to do with it."

But Doug shook his head. "Not the way Andy was talking. From what he said, I got the idea this Chuck character's been bugging her for a date."

"That wouldn't make her bawl, would it?"

"We're talking about DeeDee, remember? She doesn't have to have a reason to bawl."

Del had to admit that was true. She could be crying a storm one minute and laughing the next. Most girls seemed to be like that! But DeeDee's crying still disturbed her brothers.

"Maybe she's lonely for Sandy and Brenda. She gets that way once in a while." Del's eyes traced the shadows on the distant hills thoughtfully. "We sure can't blame her for that."

They had reached the steps of the building that housed the staff dining room.

Doug hesitated. "I hope DeeDee won't date that Grover guy."

Del really didn't know Chuck very well, but he felt the same as Doug did about him. Chuck didn't act like the kind of guy they wanted to date their sister.

"Maybe we ought to talk with her about it."

Doug shook his head. "She sure wouldn't like that!"

"I don't care. I'm going to do it anyway."

When DeeDee joined them for dinner a few minutes later, Del asked her about the date she was supposed to have the following afternoon.

Her glaring eyes focused on Del's solemn face. "And who said I had a date tomorrow?"

"You do, don't you?"

DeeDee stabbed her fork into the meat on her plate as a release for her surging temper. It wasn't enough to have Chuck bugging her every minute they were working; now Del had to butt in. "What's it to you?"

"Calm down, DeeDee." In his concern his voice was harsh and critical. "I'm just asking you about it, that's all. We just want to know."

DeeDee tilted her head and grinned smugly. "For your information, someone did ask me for a date, but that doesn't mean I'm going with him." She paused. "And it doesn't mean I'm not, either."

"We heard that Chuck Grover was going to take you with him on a trail ride tomorrow afternoon." He wanted to say more, but the warning to be silent was obvious in her hot glance.

"That's what he tried to tell me a little while ago." Her trembling fingers pushed the black hair from the gentle oval of her face. "I'm sorry to disappoint you, but I turned him down."

"I'm glad. Doug and I don't think he's the right kind of a guy for you."

"Well, thank you!" DeeDee's dark eyes glittered coldly. "Thank you so very much for your concern. I'll try to remember to ask your permission before I go out with anyone. I wouldn't want to do anything to disturb you."

Anger and hurt blazed in Del's narrowing eyes as Andy came up.

DeeDee fell silent, ashamed that she had spoken so harshly.

"Hi. Am I breaking into something?"

"We were just talking about the trail ride tomorrow." Doug was glad for the interruption.

Andy pulled out a chair and plopped into it. "Good. I thought maybe I was getting into a family argument."

DeeDee picked up her fork uneasily, wondering whether Del was going to continue the conversation or not. She would die of embarrassment if he let Andy know that he even dared to talk to her about which guys she should not date. It would be different if Danny or Kay warned her about someone. She might resent it, but they were older and responsible for her. She knew they would be thinking of her welfare.

But her brothers!

Del might have been considering her welfare too! She felt sorry that she had been so rough on him. Only she wasn't going to have him get the idea he owned her and could tell her what to do. And when it came to guys, DeeDee felt that she wasn't as stupid as Del seemed to think. Chuck was the last guy on the ranch that she would go out with. Still, she didn't want Del or Doug to tell her not to date him.

Andy was talking about something else. "Didn't you tell me you'd be going to Northwest High this year?"

"That's what Danny and Kay said."

"That's great. I just got a message from the football coach today. He reminded me to stay in condition. Says we'll have a tough job winning the league next year."

Del and Doug brightened.

"Do either of you play football?"

"Both Del and I were backs at Fairview last year."

"Yeh. We had the best team the school's ever had."

Andy shrugged indifferently. "But Fairview's such a little dump."

"Fairview's not a dump!" Del objected loyally. "We were in class B, but we played a lot of class A schools, and they didn't give us any trouble."

"Okay, so you must have had a fair team for your size," the other boy acknowledged. "But the competition we're in is something else. Why, we've got high schools with more than two thousand kids. Our junior class is probably bigger'n your whole school."

Doug frowned, his glare probing the face of the boy across the table from him. "We played a lot of big schools, and we made out all right."

Andy's grin was patronizing as he looked from one triplet to the other. "Are you guys going out for the team this year?"

"You bet we are."

"We wouldn't miss it."

Andy picked up his fork and laid it down again, precisely in the same place. "You both were regulars on your team at Fairview last year. To show you how much better we are, I'm going to make you a bet. If you go out for football at Northwest, you won't get to play enough to letter."

Del and Doug both bristled.

"You not only won't earn your letter," he continued, "you may not even survive the first squad cut."

"We'll see about that."

Suddenly DeeDee noted the time and pushed back from the table. "Sorry, I've got to run."

"We'll see you and Chuck tomorrow after lunch," Andy told her.

Her cheeks reddened, but she managed a wry smile. "Don't count on it."

With a puzzled frown on his face, Andy watched as she went out the door and hurried out of view. "What did she mean by that?"

"I thought it was plain enough," Doug said. "She's not going with Chuck on that trail ride tomorrow."

"What is it with that dumb sister of yours?" Both boys jerked upright.

"What do *you* mean by *that?*" snapped Doug.

"Don't get so uptight." He seemed surprised at Doug's reaction. "I was just thinking of what Chuck said about her. He told me she's a cute chick but a real kook when it comes to religion."

Doug placed both hands on the table and rose quickly to his feet, his piercing gaze spiking Andy to the wall. "We don't let anyone talk that way about our sister. Is that clear?"

Andy squirmed under the belligerence that had descended on him so unexpectedly. "Who's talking about your sister? I just said she's a nut on religion. That's nothin' to climb the wall about."

"I didn't like the tone of your voice." Doug was unrelenting.

"Neither did I." Del wasn't sure why Doug was

so upset, but he wasn't going to let his brother stand alone.

The other boy's eyes shifted from one triplet to the other. "Cool it, both of you. I didn't mean anything by what I said."

Doug relaxed slowly. As he thought it over, he realized that Andy hadn't said anything really so bad about DeeDee. What actually caused him to flare up was that Andy had made fun of her faith in Christ.

"I'm sorry," Doug mumbled. "Forget it."

"You must think a lot of her."

A hush stole over Doug. He never really had analyzed his feelings for DeeDee before. Not really. At last he answered, "Yeh, though most of the time she's a pain in the neck."

* * *

In their room that night Del mentioned Doug's defense of their sister. "I don't think I've ever seen you so mad. I thought you were going to clobber him right there."

"I guess I got out of line a little."

Del collapsed into a chair and flipped his shoes halfway across the room. "He got the message that he'd better be careful what he says about her, that's for sure."

Doug stood at the window, eyes searching the

darkening sky. "You know, Del, we ought to be ashamed of ourselves."

"Now what?"

"DeeDee's been sharing Christ with somebody around here, or Andy wouldn't have said what he did about her."

"I hadn't thought of it that way."

"What have you and I done about witnessing?"

Del's silence was an appropriate answer. Doug crossed the narrow room and sat down. "Andy doesn't even know we're Christians."

* * *

The next day a group of staff members saddled the horses Scot told them they could use for their excursion to the old, abandoned mining town. At first Chuck wasn't going along, but when they were about ready to leave, he changed his mind.

"Wait for me. It won't take a minute to saddle my horse."

Andy noted the time impatiently. "Okay, but snap it up. We've got to get a move on to go all the way to the ghost town and back before dark."

Chuck was grumbling to himself as he flung the saddle on his horse and tightened the cinch.

"What's eatin' you?" Andy wanted to know. "Did old Terrill give you a bad time this morning?"

"Did Terrill give *me* a bad time?" he echoed

indignantly. "You've got to be kidding. He doesn't dare say anything to me. My uncle owns this place, and I let him know it!"

"Well, there's something buggin' you. You can't kid me."

Chuck's profanity was savage. "It's that blasted girl. I get so mad at her I can't see straight."

Andy tried to change the subject, but Chuck was too wound up to talk about anything else. "I stopped to talk to her again, but she still wouldn't go out with me. She thinks she's too good for me."

By this time they had left the ranch buildings and were making their way up the crooked trail that led deep into the forest.

Andy's gaze swept Doug and Del nervously. "Forget her," he whispered. "There are lots of other girls you can go out with." Before Chuck could say anything more, he started to talk about something else.

Soon the group strung out single file to angle up the steep, coiling trail that led to the old, abandoned mining town. Andy was relieved when he saw Doug and Del take places several horses ahead. The rest of the ride passed pleasantly.

CHAPTER 8

LOOKING FOR SOMEONE?

It rained the next day, so Del and Doug were unable to work outside. They played chess and checkers until they tired of them. Then they tried a game of Monopoly for two, but that didn't work out. They read for a while, and at last Doug closed his book.

"I've about had it. What can we do?" He got up and went to the closet for his jacket. "I think I'll go over to the lodge for a while. Want to go along?"

"Old Terrill's not going to like it. Don't you remember his rules? Members of the staff are discouraged from fraternizing with the paying guests."

"I'm not going to fraternize. I'm going over to see if I can pick up a puzzle or a game of Scrabble or anything that'll keep me from going nuts trying to count the dots in the wallpaper."

"I think I'll pass."

Doug left the bunkhouse and sloshed through

the rain to the lodge. He had heard Mr. Terrill say something about some new guests coming in for the weekend, but he was completely unprepared for the encounter just inside the door. He came storming in, stamping the mud from his shoes, without looking where he was going.

"I beg your pardon!" A high-pitched, young voice stabbed through his preoccupation.

His head jerked up, and a startled gasp rose from deep within his throat.

"I–I–" He stepped back, banging the door with his heel. He almost had run into a girl about his own age – a slim, glowing blond with surprisingly familiar features and eyes that danced merrily. Somehow – he never did recall exactly what he said – somehow, he managed to apologize for his clumsiness.

She smiled forgivingly. "Haven't I seen you some-where before?"

"Well–ah–not unless you've been up here earlier this summer."

"We come often, but this is the first time this year." Then her smile flashed. "I know! You're the boy next door!"

Doug was speechless.

"Didn't you just move to Rock Point?"

"Yeh."

"That's what I thought. And I saw you and some-one I figured was your brother. You were just going up the walk when I drove up."

She *was* that girl. But it couldn't be! Doug's head spun!

Rain rattled against the windows, and the pendulum on the mantle clock loudly measured the march of the earth around the sun, second after stately second; but for Doug, time ceased to be a reality. He was transfixed by the vision of loveliness before him, captured by her impish eyes and playful smile and the flow of her soft, blond hair against her cheeks.

He had been around DeeDee's friends a great deal back in Fairview, and he rarely had experienced any difficulty in talking to them. He teased them sometimes, but for the most part he avoided them and thought they were a giggling, scatterbrained bunch. But there had never been one like the girl he was looking at now.

There probably wasn't another like her anywhere in the world. This was his chance to get acquainted, and his voice was gone. Angrily he brushed a damp hand across his face. He didn't know why he had to get so nervous he couldn't talk to her. Why couldn't he be like other guys?

His awkward plight of the moment was ended by her voice.

"I'm sorry. I didn't even introduce myself. I'm Tina Nicholson."

"And I'm Doug Davis." The words were blurted out. Not knowing what else to do, he thrust forward his hand. "I sure am glad to know you, Tina."

"It's about time we're getting acquainted, now that we're neighbors."

Slowly Doug became aware of the fact that Mr. Terrill was staring his disapproval. In a minute he would be storming over to send Doug out of the lodge and away from the attractive young guest. And there would be nothing he could do about it.

"Have you been here long?" she asked.

"I'm working here."

"How nice."

With that, Mr. Terrill left his office doorway and advanced like an arrow loosed from an archer's bow, deflecting neither to right nor left. There was no escape.

"Douglas."

"Yes, sir." He moved back half a step guiltily.

"Would you please report to Mr. MacDermott at once?" His voice was warm and casual, but there was ice in his eyes. "I'm sure he has something for you to do."

Doug nodded. He got the manager's message. Terrill wasn't putting him to work; he was stopping him from fraternizing with the guests. He turned to Tina.

"I'm sorry. I've got to go now."

"I'm so glad to get to know you."

Terrill was still there, eyes narrowed impatiently.

"I'll see you around," he said hopefully.

Her warm smile took the chill off his heart. At

least he hadn't completely turned her off. He left the building and dashed through the rain to the foreman's house. Scot was sitting at the kitchen table, his fingers caressing a steaming mug.

"Did Terrill send ye over here in this rain?"

"He said you had something for me to do."

"He must be out of his mind." Scot MacDermott weighed the matter, the lines around his eyes deepening. "But now that he sent ye, I have got something for ye to do. Come on in and take off your coat."

Doug did as he was told.

"Now, sit down an' have a cup of tea with me. I get mighty lonely on days like this."

When Doug finally got back to their room half an hour or so before dinner, Del was sitting in the same chair, eyes fixed on the same book as though he hadn't moved all afternoon.

"Where you been?" The words rumbled in his throat.

"Oh, just rapping with Scot over at his place."

Doug wanted to tell him about Tina, but he didn't dare. Del was his brother, but there were some things a guy had to keep to himself.

He crossed the room and sat down. Tina had seemed friendly enough. She just might be willing to go out with him if he ever got up nerve enough to ask her. He wondered what it would be like to have a real date alone with a girl.

* * *

The next morning at the JB ranch broke clear and warm. A brisk wind swept the sky free of clouds and rumpled the surface of a nearby lake. Doug's gaze moved restlessly across the long stretch of green that surrounded the ranch buildings as he and Del went out to the barn to work. He hoped for a glimpse of Tina Nicholson.

"Looking for someone?"

Doug's cheeks crimsoned. "Who would I be looking for?"

"I don't know, but you've sure been quiet since you were over at Scot's yesterday. And right now you act as though you're looking for a million bucks somewhere. What's the deal? Has he got a beautiful daughter stashed away in the attic?"

"Scot?" Doug hoped he sounded indignant enough to get his brother off the subject. "Don't be stupid. His daughter is married and has kids of her own!"

"Well, there's something eatin' you."

They were saddling the horses for the first trail ride of the day when Tina came out with her mother and two other girls. Doug felt the color burn in his cheeks when he saw her. He would have slipped away, but she spotted him.

"Hi, Doug." There was music in her voice.

"Hullo."

Del and Andy were watching him, amusement glittering in their eyes.

She came over to him. "Are you going to take us on the trail ride this morning?"

He shook his head. "I've got to work around here today."

"The fact is," Del broke in, "he works around here every day."

Andy snickered.

But Tina was paying no attention to them. She introduced Doug to her mother and her friends. He had no idea what their names were half a minute after they rode away, however. And he probably wouldn't even have recognized them if they rode back without her.

She liked him. She actually liked him. He read it in her smile and in the tone of her voice. He held the reins while she got on her horse, and smiled numbly as she thanked him and rode away. It wasn't real. It couldn't be.

But he was painfully aware of reality the instant Tina was gone.

Del turned to Andy. "Wow!"

"You can say that again! And just think, she knows our Douglas."

"No wonder you acted so funny when you came back to the room yesterday afternoon. Now I know what you were doing."

"I was over at Scot's," he mumbled, "just like I said."

"Maybe so, but you were somewhere else, too. You can't kid me."

"And did you notice how impressed she was?" Andy continued.

Del grinned. "You saddled that horse so nicely, Doug." His voice was a thin falsetto. "I do have to thank you. To think you got it on right side up the first time! That was so smart of you."

Doug scowled. "Lay off, will you?"

Scot had said one of them should go up to the main lodge to put a new screen on a window. Doug strode off, leaving his brother and Andy laughing uproariously.

They were just jealous, he told himself. They would like to have Tina as a friend themselves. Well, he didn't have to stand there and be laughed at.

He was a few steps from the dining room door in the lodge when it burst open and DeeDee rushed out. He could see that she was crying. He dashed forward and caught her roughly by the arm, pulling her to a stop.

"What's the matter?"

She did not answer him.

"What is it? DeeDee, what happened?"

She did not answer him immediately. Her head was turned, hiding her tear-stained face. "Please, Doug. Leave me alone."

"Not until you tell me what this is all about."

Slowly she turned toward him and raised her

head. She had stopped crying, but anger still smoldered in her eyes.

"It's nothing. Nothing at all."

"Now don't give me that. I know better."

"But I tell you it isn't anything." She blinked rapidly as though she was about to cry again. "It's just that I get so mad at that Chuck Grover. He keeps tormenting me and won't stop until he has me so upset, I'm bawling."

Doug frowned and drew in a deep breath. "I'm going to have to talk to that character."

"Please don't! That will only make him worse. I can handle it okay."

"You may be able to handle it, but you're not going to do it alone. I'm not having my sister pushed around by Chuck Grover or anyone else. He's got to get that into his pointed little head."

His determination to defend her amazed DeeDee. She had never seen him that way before.

"But I have to work with him the rest of the summer. I don't want you to say anything to him." She wiped her eyes and put on a brave little smile. "I'll be all right. Don't worry about it."

"Who's worried? I'm going to see him and make him understand he's got to leave you alone."

"Promise you won't go to him about–about my being upset by his teasing, Doug. There's no reason for you to have trouble with him. I can handle it."

"I'm not promising anything."

"I don't see why you have to be so stubborn," she flared.

"You're my sister and I just happen to care about you." He sounded embarrassed at admitting it. "What kind of a guy would I be if I let some stupid character like Chuck give you a bad time?"

DeeDee decided it was useless to try to convince him that she didn't want him to go to Chuck. Actually, she found it pleasing. It was good to know he thought so much of her that he wasn't going to let anyone bother her. And Del would be the same, she was sure. Some girls were fortunate to have one brother. She had two to look out for her.

Sometimes they made her so mad she wished she didn't have any brothers, but they were nice to have around after all. It gave her a feeling of security to know that Doug cared enough to do something if she really needed it.

CHAPTER 9

IT'S GOT TO STOP

Doug went into the dining room where Chuck was clearing tables.

The slight, hawk-faced lad looked up. "Hi Doug. Lookin' for someone?"

He nodded, eyes cold and lips tightened into a thin line.

"Tina-baby went out for a while, so you're out of luck."

The remark caught Doug by surprise. "How do you know about Tina?"

"Oh, come on! I saw you two talking in the lodge yesterday. Made sure watchdog Terrill saw you too." Chuck grinned archly. "Did he give you a bad time?"

Doug smothered his anger and ignored the question. "What time do you get off work?"

"In twenty or thirty minutes. Why?"

"I want to talk to you when you get through." Doug's hostility seeped through.

"What're you so uptight about? I haven't done anything to you. Besides, ol' Terrill has to be kept on his toes."

"I'll talk to you when you get off work."

Chuck snorted defensively. "Now, don't think you can get funny with me. My uncle happens to own this place."

Doug glared at him. "I don't care if your uncle owns half the state. I still want to talk to you when you get off work."

"Okay. Okay. We'll talk when I get off work, but you don't have to get so mad about it."

Doug whirled around and strode away, fists clenched at his sides. Chuck stared after him.

Doug stormed out of the long building, ignoring the warmth of the summer sun and the wind that was whispering through the pines and aspen in the ranch yard. Anger frosted the color from his cheeks and narrowed his black eyes. He should have grabbed Chuck by the collar in the dining room so everyone who had heard him taunting DeeDee would know what was happening to him. That was what he deserved. Then, maybe he would stop to think before he picked on another girl.

Despite the hostility that surged over him, Doug knew that he had to control himself, at least in consideration of DeeDee.

Doug waited nervously. He had work to do, but at the moment this was more important. He had to have it out with Chuck now. He couldn't allow him to bother his sister anymore.

After a while, he looked at his watch and glanced at the door Chuck would be using to leave the building. The other boy had been scared when he left him in the dining room, as scared as a rabbit with a fox on his tail. He just might try to get out of the building without Doug seeing him.

Well, that would not work. Not with him, it wouldn't. With affected carelessness he sauntered toward the door. Just let Chuck try to slip away. He would nail him before he got twenty yards.

Doug was only a few short paces from the door when Chuck came out. He started when he saw the Davis boy.

He had been planning to try to sneak to his room. Doug could tell by his uneasy smile and the sweat that beaded his forehead.

"I thought you were going to wait for me out back," Chuck mumbled.

"I changed my mind."

"Well, here I am. Start rappin'. I've got a date this afternoon, and I don't want to keep a cute little chick waitin'."

Doug led him to the parking lot some distance from the lodge.

"You've been giving DeeDee a bad time ever since

we got here." His voice was low and well controlled, but his hostility was obvious.

"Come off it! I was just having a little fun, that's all. Don't let it throw you."

"It's got to stop."

Chuck's lips pouted mockingly. "Who do you think you're scaring?"

"If it happens again, you'll have to answer to me! Just remember that!"

At that moment Del came running.

"Hey, Doug, Scot's been lookin' all over for you. He–" His throat caught the words and trapped them in midsentence. "What's goin' on?"

"Chuck and I are having a little talk about DeeDee. He's been giving her a bad time."

Del's young face became as stern as his brother's. "If that happens again, you'll have to answer to both Doug and me!"

Chuck's gaze shifted from one triplet to the other as they towered over him. "I–I didn't mean nothin' by it."

"You think about that the next time you get any bright thoughts about teasing her," Doug said firmly.

Del and Doug stepped back and allowed the shaken youth to hurry away toward the staff bunkhouse. There was nothing more they could do about him.

"I think that'll be the end of it," Del said. "He's plenty scared."

"You never can tell what a guy like Chuck will

do. He's somethin' else." Doug's eyes narrowed and his fists clenched. "He'd better leave her alone – and mind his own business. That's all I can say."

At five o'clock the boys left the horse sheds and ambled across the yard, still thinking about Chuck Grover. They were halfway to the lodge when Mr. Terrill came out of the side door and hurried toward them.

"Have you seen Charles?" Consternation colored his voice – and face.

At first, they didn't know what he was talking about.

"Charles Grover, Mr. Kramer's nephew. No one has seen him all afternoon."

Mr. Terrill was obviously agitated. He pranced closer to Doug and Del, his quick, nervous glance shuttling from one to the other. "Someone said he saw you boys talking to Charles."

"That was early this morning. We haven't seen him since then."

Mr. Terrill's narrow black moustache quivered. "Charles was disturbed at noon. Hardly talked to anyone. Now it's almost time for dinner, and I haven't been able to find him."

"Want us to help you look?" Del asked.

"We've got to find him!" Anger darkened the manager's eyes. "I don't know why these things always have to happen to me. Here I am with a capacity crowd and a thousand problems. If Charles weren't Mr. Kramer's nephew, I'd discharge him this afternoon."

Doug and Del left Mr. Terrill and headed toward the horse sheds to search for Chuck.

"You don't suppose our little talk caused him to run away, do you?"

"All we did was tell him to leave DeeDee alone."

"Maybe he was scared we both were going to jump on him and give him a beating."

They checked the horse sheds and walked through the barn, but there was no sign of Chuck. Neither Scot nor Andy had seen him since noon. Nor had any of the other hands.

"Come on, Del." Doug turned away from the others. "We'd better get up to the lodge and tell Mr. Terrill we couldn't find him."

Del's lean legs stretched to full length as they hurried across the lawns. "He just might pull a trick, like hiding out somewhere, and think it was a great joke."

The boys didn't have to look for Mr. Terrill. He sought them out, swooping from his office in the main lodge to corner them.

"We looked all over for Chuck, but we weren't able to find him."

"That's not surprising." His gaze was a sword thrust through Doug. "I understand you two had some trouble with Charles this morning."

They squirmed uncomfortably. "Not exactly. We just told him to quit bothering our sister."

"And you both threatened him!"

"We didn't do that." Doug spoke defensively, trying to explain what had taken place.

The manager scarcely listened. "We'll discuss this matter more fully after Charles is found."

"But–"

"Don't think the matter is closed. I intend to deal with both of you most severely as soon as I have time." He gestured widely with his hands. "A staff of twenty-five people and you had to pick out Mr. Kramer's nephew to bully!"

Numbly they watched him flutter away.

"We are in for it now!" Del exclaimed.

Doug moved across the narrow hall to the big window that overlooked the lower slope and the valley beyond. It was obvious the dude ranch manager already had made up his mind that the boys were responsible for Chuck's disappearance.

"And we'll probably be in bad with Mr. Kramer, too," Doug added numbly.

Mr. Terrill came bustling back to inform them that one of the saddle horses and Chuck's bedroll and gear were gone. "Who knows where he would have gone?" Terrill waved his arms in desperation. "He could have gone anywhere. And with a four-hour head start! I should have stayed in Pittsburgh."

"Are you going to call the sheriff?" Doug asked.

At the mention of the authorities, Terrill's cheeks went sallow, and horror gleamed in his eyes.

"It wouldn't be good for business if people found

out that one of our staff had disappeared." His little black moustache bobbed in consternation. "I've tried hard to be a good manager for Mr. Kramer." He was talking to no one in particular. "If I live through this summer, I'll never take the job again."

"Can we help you?" Del offered anxiously.

He gulped a quick breath. "Yes, yes, there is something you can do." He lowered his voice as a couple of guests approached. "Go out to Mr. MacDermott and tell him what has happened. Tell him I want the matter handled promptly but discreetly. Understand?"

They started to hurry away, but Terrill called them back.

"And whatever you do, warn him not to say anything that will alarm the guests. We want the people to think of the JB ranch as a place of rest and tranquility."

The boys ran to do as they were told.

Scot was not dismayed by the news that Chuck was missing.

"That kid's been too big for his britches ever since he got here. Well, I guess we'd better go out and look for him."

For all of his calmness, Scot moved swiftly to organize a search party for the missing boy. He divided the staff into pairs and assigned them areas to cover.

"And we'd better get with it. It's not going to be long until dark." He squinted at the clouds that were rolling among the peaks. "And, if he went up, we're apt to have some snow to contend with before we find him. It 'pears to me that there's going to be a storm on the ridge before morning."

Scot's quiet forecast of the weather chilled Doug and Del. They had had no experience with snow in the mountains, but they had been in plenty of blizzards in Minnesota. It wasn't the kind of weather a guy would care to be lost in.

Del and Doug were encouraged when they found that the horses they used to own were in the barn. They saddled them quickly and were about to ride off when they decided to stop by the kitchen for some sandwiches to take along.

DeeDee came in with an order while the boys were waiting. She rushed over to them. "I heard about Chuck, and I feel terrible. It was all my fault."

"Don't say that," Del told her. "If he'd left you alone, we wouldn't have said anything to him."

"That's right," Doug added. "And if he'd paid attention to what we told him, he wouldn't have chased off. We didn't threaten him. We just told him to leave you alone or he would have to answer to us."

"But he's gone now. And it is supposed to snow in the hills tonight."

The cook brought their sandwiches.

"I'll be praying for Chuck," DeeDee whispered, "and for both of you."

Before leaving the ranch yard, Del and Doug bowed their heads and asked God to help someone find Chuck before the night was over. They rode out of the yard and through a cattle gate in the direction of the high pastures.

The sun had lost its footing on the mountaintop and slipped behind the ridge, deepening the shadows and sending long, gray fingers across both meadows and timberland. The eastern horizon was hidden by clouds, great rolling billows eager to race across the sky.

"It sure does look as though it's going to snow," Doug said.

His brother shivered and zipped his jacket together. "Feels like it, too."

Doug reached down and touched the switch on the electric lantern he had tied to the saddle horn. "I sure wish we had some idea of where to look."

"Scot thinks he's headed for Rock Point," Doug commented. "I guess he threatened to leave the ranch and go home a couple of times when he got mad at somebody earlier in the summer."

Del reined up suddenly and pointed at a hoof print just ahead. "Somebody's been along here on a horse within the last few hours."

Doug laughed dryly. "This is a ranch, remember? And there must be at least fifty horses around the place. No matter what direction you go, you'll find hoof prints."

Del brushed a strand of black hair from his forehead. It was hopeless to try to track down a single horse. How would they ever find Chuck Grover?

CHAPTER 10

WHERE ARE YOU?

Del and Doug urged their mounts across a slender mountain stream that was racing noisily for the valley, pushed across a narrow stretch of cedar and aspen, and angled up the steep pastureland. Darkness was reaching out for them, and the chill wind stung their faces and stiffened their fingers on the reins. As they rode, they spoke very little.

Doug twisted half around to eye his brother questioningly. "We're just riding along without any idea where we're going."

"We're covering the territory Scot lined out for us."

"But we still don't know where we're to look exactly. Have you any idea where he could have gone, except down to the city?"

Frowning, Del shook his head. "How could anyone know what a guy like that would do? Anyway, I don't think he went to town."

"I've been wondering about that myself. I don't think he likes to ride that well."

"And I don't think he split because he was so afraid of you and me. We didn't get that rough with him."

Doug had reached the same conclusion. He hadn't liked Chuck, but he had to admit the guy was smart enough to know that Doug and Del weren't going to give him a beating. No, there had to be another reason for his disappearance.

Doug changed hands on the reins and stuffed his cold fingers into his jacket pocket. Whatever the reason, Chuck had sure put them in bad with old Terrill. Suddenly he stood upright in the stirrups. "I think I've got it!"

"Got what? Frostbite?"

"I think Chuck knew Mr. Terrill would find out that you and I had him cornered this morning. I've a hunch he's hiding out somewhere just to get us into trouble."

Del drew in a deep breath. "That makes sense."

"The question is what do we do about it?"

* * *

DeeDee waited tables in the dining room that evening, but her mind was not on her work. It seemed that the minutes crawled by. Night rode in on a rising wind – a gloomy night without stars or moon, an oppressive night weighed down with apprehension.

She worked woodenly, taking orders and serving her guests with mechanical efficiency. When Del and Doug rode away to search for Chuck Grover, she had been sure she could not stay on the job another moment; but she had had no choice. Mr. Terrill was depending on her; there was nothing else for her to do. And besides, he insisted that everything go on as normal as possible. Once the search party was gone, he had called the dining room staff together for a whispered conference, telling them what had taken place and the course of action he and Scot MacDermott were following.

"Now, remember." He had sounded close to hysteria. "Remember that everything is to go on as though nothing has happened. Even though Charles is gone and we don't know where he is or whether he'll be found, we must not alarm our guests. Is that clear?"

Murmured assent had drifted from one to the other in the big room.

"If certain people had been more considerate, we would not be faced with this problem tonight." His scathing glare had found DeeDee. "But that was not the case, so we are faced with a most serious situation."

She had squirmed miserably. Mr. Terrill didn't have to be so cruel. She felt bad enough about it as it was. She was responsible for Chuck's running away. If anything happened to him, it would be her fault.

Mr. Terrill had dismissed them as quickly as he

had called them together, ordering them back to their posts.

Somehow DeeDee managed to get through the dinner hour. She got a couple of orders mixed and almost spilled coffee on a guest, but time passed, and finally she served her last meal. She had tried hard to keep from showing her concern, but she was sure that at least some of those she waited on knew that there was something wrong. An elderly, graying man had asked her about it.

"What's the matter, DeeDee? You act as though you're the most miserable person in Colorado. Did you have a fight with your boyfriend?"

To deny she was disturbed would be to lie, and to tell what was actually bothering her would violate Mr. Terrill's edict and make things even worse than they were already. The only response she could give was a quiet smile.

At last the evening was over. As soon as she finished clearing the tables, she went to her room and knelt in prayer, asking God to take care of Del and Doug and to help someone to find Chuck Grover.

* * *

Del was staring at his brother. "How about it? Do we go back and tell Mr. Terrill we're sure Chuck is hiding out to get us into trouble?"

"He'd never believe us. And besides, we'd lose a lot

of valuable time. We'd better keep right on hunting for Chuck until we've covered our territory."

They rode on.

After several minutes Del sputtered excitedly, "The old ghost town!"

"What?"

"I don't know why we didn't think of it before. If Chuck was looking for a place to hide, what better place could he find than the old ghost town?"

The boys urged their mounts forward, excitement growing with each step of their wiry, sure-footed cow ponies. At the fork in the trail, they turned left, climbing up the steep ridge in the direction of the deserted mining town.

They were wrapped in darkness now, so thick it almost hid one from the other. Snow was in the air. It stung their cheeks and clung to their wool jackets. Slowly they made their way up the narrow, twisting trail to the town that died with the end of the silver boom more than a century before.

"Now, if Chuck's around here, we ought to be able to find him pronto." Del raised his voice against the whine of the wind. "Where are you? Chuck Grover! Where are you?"

No answer.

He called again, louder this time, but still without success.

"That isn't going to do any good," Doug said at last. "He couldn't hear you thirty feet away." He paused. "Besides, if I know him, he's going to hide if he does hear us. He's not going to come out and let us find him."

They advanced slowly, stopping to dismount at each decrepit building. Doug entered warily, the electric lantern in his hand, to probe the dusty innards of the abandoned stores and dwellings. But there was no sign of Chuck or his horse.

The boys worked their way up the single street, building by building. They went through several houses, from one room to another, and on to the old hotel, the general store, and the saloon. There was evidence that people had been there recently, but no one was around at the moment. There was no sign of Chuck or his saddle horse.

There were two buildings left when they paused for a quick conference.

"What do you think?"

"Chuck must not be here." Doug did not even try to mask his disappointment. "If he were, we'd have found him by this time for sure."

"Maybe he heard us and kept moving ahead of us."

Doug grunted in disgust. "There was no sign of anyone having been in any of the buildings today." He cleared his throat. "Nope, I think we must've missed it. I don't see how he could have come up here at all."

They listened to the whistling of the wind as it shook the old buildings and tap-danced against the loose shutters. Doug was in favor of turning back, but Del insisted they go through the last two buildings.

"It'll only take a couple of minutes. Then we'll know that we've checked out everything."

The first building was empty. As they started toward the last one, a shrill whinny pierced the noise of the wind.

Del grabbed his brother by the arm. "Did you hear that?"

"A horse! And it wasn't one of ours!"

The mountain storm was all about them. It whipped the scrawny trees and scattered snow along the empty street, a blustery reminder that winter in the high places was not far away.

The horse whinnied again, a plaintive bugling that sounded above the cold wind. Del's mount answered the eerie cry.

Doug grabbed his brother by the arm. "Somebody is here!"

"Maybe Scot sent someone else this way!"

But Doug didn't think so. "He was plain about wanting us to take this area. He wouldn't have sent anyone else up here with so much ground to cover elsewhere." He moved to his left a few hesitant steps, listening intently. "It isn't one of the hands. It's got to be Chuck!"

At the edge of the building where the wind could reach them with its savage spears, Doug stopped. "What's the use of looking for the horse? Chuck isn't going to be outside. He's going to be in one of the buildings if he's around."

With that they turned and advanced to the front door of the only building they had not searched. The flashlight punched an eerie, yellow hole in the night, the slender shaft of light picking out an old sofa sagging against the wall, a chair with no seat, and a broken rocker. Glass from a lamp chimney was scattered across the dust-carpeted floor, and a piece of picture frame still lay on a windowsill where it must have been used to prop open the sash on a long-past summer afternoon. Quickly the light swept the narrow room, but there was no evidence that anyone had been inside the building in days. The thick coat of dirt was undisturbed, save for the tracks of the rats that had taken over.

Disappointment groaned from Doug's lips. "He hasn't even been here!"

"Maybe he heard us and took off."

"In this storm? He'd have to be out of his ever-loving mind to ride away from a building at night in a storm like this."

They continued their search, desperation growing. The bedrooms and the kitchen were as empty as the living room had been. The scattered remains of the former occupants' dreams were still there in the form of furniture and cooking utensils too badly battered or broken to be worth stealing. But Chuck was not there. And there were no footprints to show that he had even been around.

Doug paused once more. "We did hear a horse outside a little while ago, didn't we?" he asked, his voice rising in doubt.

"I sure thought so."

"I hope we did. I'm beginning to think I'm the one who's goin' out of his mind."

At that moment there was a hush in the storm – a tense, expectant pause as though the wind had to catch its breath. During the lull, a faint groan drifted to them.

The boys stared at each other, listening intently.

The wind came up once more, as swiftly as it died away but not before they heard the sound of groaning again.

"There *is* someone out there!" Del cried excitedly. "And he must be in trouble!"

The boys dashed forward and flung the kitchen door open. Del was about to rush into the enclosed back porch, but Doug's warning cry stopped him. "Watch it, Del!"

A great, black hole gaped at them from the floor! They inched through the door, approaching the hole with care until they could see the crumpled figure of a person lying in the cellar beneath.

Del's voice broke above the sound of the wind. "Chuck!"

CHAPTER 11

SHE IS PRAYING FOR YOU

At the sound of his name, the figure below stirred feebly.

Doug flashed his light around the porch, but he could find no stairway to the basement.

"Here!" Del squatted beside the hole, grasped an exposed two-by-four with both hands, and swung his feet over the edge to drop to the dirt floor beside Chuck.

Doug tossed the big lantern down to him and lowered himself to the basement floor.

"Chuck!" Del cried, bending over the injured lad. "What happened?"

The boy on the floor opened his eyes, and his lips parted wordlessly. Then Doug noticed that Chuck's leg was doubled grotesquely under him.

He pointed in horror. "It's his leg!"

Chuck managed to murmur in agreement.

"It's broken, Doug."

"I can see that!" The words were harsh and irritable. "But what're we going to do? We can't take him out of here on horseback, that's for sure."

The injured boy grimaced as pain throbbed up his leg. "There's–" His throat constricted, chopping off the sentence with the first word.

"What is it, Chuck? What're you trying to say?" Doug leaned over the fallen boy.

"The road goes – down to–"

"I think he's trying to tell us about the road that comes up here."

Chuck fought the pain until he was able to go on. "There's a road down to the highway. It – goes the long way around, but–"

Doug did not allow him to continue. "That's it! As soon as daylight comes, one of us can ride down and tell Mr. Terrill. He can send the car up here."

Chuck frowned his disagreement. "Jeep."

"Scot will know whether the car can make it up here or if he'll have to send the jeep," Del assured him.

Doug and Del helped Chuck get as comfortable as possible. Taking the lantern, they found the cellar stairs and went out to where Chuck's horse was tied.

While Doug unbuckled the bedroll, Del went to get their horses. Snow was already caking along their sleek flanks.

"I'll take the horses around to that lean-to near the back porch. It'll protect them from this wind, and they can bunch together to keep warm." Del tugged at the reins.

A couple of minutes later Doug was beside Chuck. He wrapped him in the blankets and put a spare shirt under his head. Getting warm seemed to ease the pain slightly. Haltingly, he told Doug about leaving the ranch and riding up to the ghost town. They had been right about his wanting to get them into trouble.

Del came down the stairs, shaking snow off of his jacket. "Why did you do it? That's what we want to know."

Chuck looked aside petulantly and said no more until Doug asked him to go on.

"What happened then?"

"I–I was going to stop in this house for the night. I'd looked in here a couple of days ago on our trail ride and knew there was a stove here. But what I didn't know was that the back porch floor had almost rotted away. I stepped on it and broke through. Down I went!" He shuddered.

"I–I didn't know how long I was going to have to lie down here before anyone came and–and found me!"

"We can thank God we did come this way."

"And we can thank Him that your horse whinnied when he did," added Doug. "I was all for turning back without checking this house. If we'd done that, we wouldn't have found you."

Chuck lay back and closed his eyes. "You sound like that sister of yours." Disgust honed his voice. "She was always talking about praying and that sort of stuff, too."

"She is praying for you," Del said simply and factually.

"You've got to be kidding."

"That's the truth." Doug added his testimony to Del's. "DeeDee's been praying for you, and so have we."

Chuck's laugh was thin and derisive. He turned his face away from them and refused to talk anymore. Finally, he closed his eyes and slept fitfully. The pain was still there. He tried to ignore it, but occasionally he groaned aloud and moved an arm or his uninjured leg.

Doug and Del prayed quietly before trying to sleep. They thanked God for leading them to the house where Chuck had fallen, and they asked Him to help them get back to the ranch in the morning and to enable a vehicle to make it up to the ghost town to take the injured boy to the hospital.

The night passed slowly, the light of their watches marking off the minutes, then hours. Shortly after midnight, when all three were awake, Chuck asked them about prayer.

"Why were you guys praying for me?" he demanded.

Doug sat up to answer him. "Because we're concerned about you."

Chuck's lips parted as he cleared his throat before speaking. "I figured you'd want to kick me in the teeth."

"We just wanted to stop you from picking on DeeDee, that's all." Del's voice reached him through the darkness. "We haven't anything against you personally."

"If she hadn't kept buggin' me, I wouldn't have given her such a bad time," Chuck said defensively. "But she was always on my back."

"Just exactly what do you mean by that?" Del demanded.

"She kept at me about that religion of hers." Chuck snorted scornfully. "Tellin' me how wonderful it would be if I would only let Jesus Christ be my Savior. She had me so uptight I couldn't even sleep at night." His lips curled. "So, don't give me such a bad time about the way I pestered her. She's the one who started it."

Doug stared at the dim outline of the hole above them. So that was what had caused the trouble between DeeDee and Chuck. She had been witnessing to him about the Lord, and he was so antagonistic that he lashed back at her.

"But DeeDee wasn't trying to pick on you. She is so happy in her life with Jesus Christ that she wants to share Him with those who work with her."

Del started to speak also but stopped so his brother could continue.

"Jesus will save you from your sin if you confess that you're a sinner and put your trust in Him to save you so you can go to heaven."

Del broke in. "And He'll help you to live a Christian life and to be happier than you've ever been before."

Chuck's breathing was slow and measured. "You two can be kooks about religion if you want to, but you'd just as well quit workin' on me. I'm not buyin' it!"

The rest of the night wore itself away gradually, like a rock being worn by the endless dripping of water. Chuck had remained silent, gripped in the vise of pain. Doug and Del were quiet too, numbed by the weariness that swept over them but too miserable to sleep soundly.

With the coming of the first gray streaks of daylight, Del stirred, then stood up and stretched his cramped limbs.

Doug opened his eyes. "What's the matter?"

"I thought I'd see what the weather's like. One of us has to go down to the ranch and get some help up here for Chuck."

With the coming of morning, the storm lost much of its vigor. The wind was exhausted from its night of roistering and crept off to bed, kicking feebly at the last flakes of falling snow. Del's boots crunched through a small snowdrift that had formed by the lean-to where the ponies were sheltered. He tightened the girth of his mount's saddle, untied him, and swung up.

It was a long ride down the narrow trail now slippery with new snow, but he was on a surefooted western pony that had been bred and trained in rugged country. The sun was boring holes in the scattered clouds and beginning to melt the snow. By the time Del reached the ranch, the snow was gone.

Mr. Terrill saw him ride up and rushed out to meet him. "Don't tell me that brother of yours is missing too!" Anguish wrung his voice. His face was haggard from lack of sleep.

"No, it's nothing like that. He stayed with Chuck."

Mr. Terrill stared incredulously at him. "You don't mean to tell me that you found him?"

"He was in the basement of an old house in the ghost town. He'd fallen through the porch floor."

"You aren't teasing me about that, are you?"

"I wouldn't have left Doug back there if I were teasing you, would I?" In spite of himself, pity crept into his voice.

"I–I just can't believe it." It was a moment or two before he could speak again. "I thought I would have to tell Mr. Kramer that his nephew was lost and we hadn't been able to find him!"

Mr. Terrill rushed off toward the room of their only doctor guest. A minute or two later the two of them jumped into the ranch car and careened out of the yard.

Del had wanted to go back with them, but Mr. Terrill was so flustered that he drove off without him.

* * *

While Doug and Chuck waited in the cellar of the abandoned house, Doug tried once more to talk with his companion about his need of Christ. "You're somethin' else!" Chuck lashed at him irritably. "Here I am with a busted leg and hurtin' so bad I can hardly stand it, and what do you do? You try to preach at me! You're worse than that stupid sister of yours."

"I don't mean to make you mad, Chuck, but–"

"Then shut up and leave me alone!" He closed his eyes tightly.

Doug tried to talk with him about other things, but he remained in tight-lipped misery until Mr. Terrill arrived with the doctor. A few minutes later the doctor had given Chuck a shot to help ease the pain and splinted his leg so the fracture wouldn't be compounded when he was moved.

"Now, if you two will help me, we'll get him out to the car."

"Is–is it going to hurt much when you move me?"

"We'll be as careful as we can."

As soon as the car pulled out of the abandoned town and was on its way to the Rock Point hospital, Doug got the horses and headed toward the ranch. A certain uneasiness dogged him all the way back. He didn't know why Chuck had to be so contrary when they tried to share Christ with him. He acted as though they were trying to force him into something.

But Doug had to admit he and Del had been really poor witnesses for Jesus Christ there at the ranch. He decided that during the rest of the summer he would let the other guys know he was a Christian. He prayed that God would help him to use his opportunities wisely.

CHAPTER 12

WE'VE GOT TO DO A LOT BETTER

Mr. Terrill and the doctor took Chuck to the hospital where his leg was set and put in a cast. He thought he was going to be released in time to start school, but such was not the case. The teenager was still in the hospital when Danny and Kay went up to the ranch to get the triplets.

The boys hadn't gone to the hospital to see Chuck. During the drive back to Rock Point, Danny urged them to do so.

"I had a call from Mr. Kramer today. He said Chuck's had some complications with his leg and is still in the hospital."

Doug nodded. "We know."

"He thought it would be nice if you boys would go see him. He thinks maybe he'll listen to the gospel now."

"Maybe I should go, too," offered DeeDee. "I

really don't want to, but in a way, I feel responsible for what happened."

"Forget it," Del assured her. "Did we tell you what he told us about running off to the ghost town to hide? He let the fact that we had cornered him leak to Mr. Terrill, then he sneaked up to the old mine and hid so he'd get us into trouble. He figured Mr. Terrill would get mad at us and fire us."

"I know." She gazed back at the mountains fading into the distance. "If only he would have listened to me when I talked with him about his need for Jesus Christ. That's what's wrong: he doesn't know God."

Del and Doug glanced at each other uneasily. What she said was true. "The worst of it is," Del confessed, "Doug and I didn't do anything to help you."

"What do you mean?"

"We didn't let him or anyone else know we're Christians too. You had to do all the witnessing yourself."

"It might not have made any difference," she said.

"Maybe not, but we didn't even try until Chuck was gone and the summer was practically over."

* * *

The following afternoon the boys went to the hospital to see Chuck. Andy and a friend were just leaving when they got there.

"Well, if it isn't the Jesus boys!" Andy greeted them as they passed by in the corridor.

Del and Doug looked at each other apprehensively. The door to Chuck's room was open.

"Well, if it isn't my dear uncle's own personal missionaries! Come in and pull up a pulpit."

They entered but with some uneasiness. Chuck, who had been sitting up when they came in, pulled himself higher in bed and let his narrowing gaze drift from one to the other. His belligerence was poorly hidden behind a transparent smile.

"Well, go ahead. Let's get it over with."

They didn't know what he meant and told him so.

"Now don't give me that. You came here to preach to me. Well, go ahead."

The boys had already experienced times when a guy would ridicule them for witnessing to him, but it always was hard to take.

"We really would like to talk with you about Jesus Christ, Chuck," Del said. He went on to explain the plan of salvation simply and carefully.

When he paused, Doug took up the theme, telling Chuck what Jesus Christ had done for them, how he helped them during that awful period following the death of their parents, and how He led Danny and Kay to take them in so all three could stay together.

Chuck Grover listened intently, then interrupted with a scoffing snarl. "That may be all right for you, but what could it do for me? Stow it! I don't want to hear any more!"

"But–"

"You came here to preach to me, so now you can leave. I'm not buyin' it! I'd heard plenty of that stuff long before you or that sister of yours ever came around. Forget it! It's not gonna get to me!"

Chuck pointed toward the open door. "Go on. Go talk to someone who appreciates your preaching to them."

There was nothing for the boys to do but leave.

When they were outside in the warm autumn sunshine, Del grinned ruefully. "I guess it didn't do much good to witness to him. He was really out to cut us down!"

Doug reached up to pluck a yellow leaf. "It would have been great if he had made a decision for Christ, but as far as we're concerned, that isn't the most important thing."

"It isn't?" His brother eyed him curiously. "You'll have to explain that to me."

"The important thing is that we talked to him about Jesus Christ. In spite of the way he ordered us out, I'm glad we talked to him. Aren't you?"

Del nodded. "I get what you mean. We did what we had to do, even though it was pretty rough."

"Chuck didn't accept Christ this time, but God will keep on using His Word to convict him. And we had a part in it."

Together the two boys strode down the street toward a nearby bus stop.

"Only, from now on, we've got to do a lot better." Doug's fist was clenched in determination.

THE
DANNY ORLIS
SERIES

The Danny Orlis series, by Bernard Palmer, delivers a blend of adventure, mystery, and suspense through various settings—from the Canadian wilderness to Guatemalan jungles. Danny Orlis, an adept outdoorsman, skilled athlete, and committed Christian, employs his quick thinking, calm bravery, and biblical solutions to confront everyday problems and hair-raising dangers. Early stories focus on Danny navigating school life, sports, and outdoor challenges, while in later books, Danny and his wife Kay provide wisdom and guidance to youngsters facing lifelike situations and challenges. Having sold over two million copies, this series has made Palmer a renowned author in Christian youth literature. Palmer is also the author of the Felicia Cartright series and various other series for Christian youth.

AVAILABLE FROM WWW.ANEKOPRESS.COM

9 798889 360780